SKIN TESTS

"IN THE MIDST OF WINTER, I FINALLY LEARNED THAT THERE WAS IN ME AN INVINCIBLE SUMMER."

–ALBERT CAMUS

SKIN TESTS

SHORT SHORT FICTION

KEN RIVARD

BLACK MOSS PRESS

2000

Published by Black Moss Press at 2450 Byng Road, Windsor, Ontario N8W 3E8. Black Moss books are distributed by Firefly Books in Canada and the U.S.

Black Moss would like to acknowledge the support of the Canada Council for the Arts for its publishing program.

Financial assistance was also provided by the Ontario Arts Council.

Cover design by John Doherty
Cover photograph by Marty Gervais

Canadian Cataloguing In Publication Data

Rivard, Ken, 1947—
  Skin tests

ISBN 0-88753-337-X

  1. Title.

PS8585.18763S58 2000   C813'.54   C00-900564-1
PR9199.3.R5256S58 2000

Acknowledgements
Many of these pieces appeared in their original forms in: *Arc, Antigonish Review, Contemporary Verse 2, Dalhousie Review, Fiddlehead, Germination, Nebula, New Quarterly, Prairie Fire, Prism International, Queen's Quarterly, Sanscrit, Wascana Review* and *Waves.* Thanks to Mick Burrs and Richard Harrison for their suggestions and to Robert Hilles for being such a great friend. This book is for H.P. and for my daughter, Annie's and her chocolate eyes of eternal optimism.

TABLE OF CONTENTS

I. UP GROWING

Pocket Crest   11
Bubbles And Ice   12
Crutches   13
Because Of The Sun's Grace   14
The Priest, The Mother   15
First Red Traffic Light   16
How The Wolf Became A Collie   17
Gina   18
Clearasil Chins   19
Pretending To Be Dead   20
Seeing Death Perform Like It Does   21

II. NOT IN MY OWN SKIN

Color   25
Name   26
Mole Removal   27
Cartoon   28
Furnace   29
In This Town Of Crepe Paper Sun   31
Road   32
The Shapes Are Gentle Questions   33
Winning Trees   34
That Bright Or That Dark   35
Scratching On The Cranium   36
Sixty Then Ninety   38

III. REPORTER

Lepers   41
From A Holy Roman Skull Factory   42
Whiskey On White   43

Except For Bees   44
Pirates And Morons   45
Fast Ones   47
Bingo And Sex   49
Music Recital   50
Timing   51
Betty Ann Picks A Card   52
Hanging As A Droplet Of Rain   54
Temperature   55
Cree Moment   56
Crayons   57
Smoke And Angel Hair   58
The Ostrich Wears Glasses   59
Monkey Puzzle   60
Light Breathing   6`

IV. TRADES

Vegetables And The Butcher   65
The Pink Carousel Horse   66
Scream   67
Holiday Fingers   68
Two Cents On Hunting   69
Ballad Of The Tin Can   70
Head Uglies   71
Boxes, Booze, Flowers, Stamps   72
A Cast   73
The Fire Will Not Wait   74
Sorting   75

V. NIGHT NET

What The Heart Might Have Done   78
On The Numbers   80
Beasts And Babies   81
Living Help   82
Spaghetti, Keyholes, Sammy   83

Waterton Lake Highway Woman   84

So What If Gophers Skipped On Her Skirts   85

Inkblot   86

Lawn Chairs And The Party   87

After The Kill   88

Sentences   89

Night Net   90

The Lines Of Arlene   92

Everyone Has A Large Intestine   93

Pure   95

And The Day After That   96

Five Skins Of Europe   97

In The Church Of Hands And Laughter   106

Sonata   108

I
UP GROWING

POCKET CREST

"Wake up! Wake up!" my stepmother screams or my stepfather yells. I have to feed my year-old sister. Change her diaper. Place her back in the crib so gently she doesn't know it's happening. Then I'd better go back to sleep. Or else! That's when I put on my favorite shirt, the one made for my skin.

Today, on my ninth birthday, I am wearing my cherished green shirt with an ESSO crest above the pocket. I have no choice but to take care of anyone younger than myself. I know nothing else. Last week I remember my stepmother saying:

"You've got so much determination on your face that I bet you're the kind of kid who will plan a simple death for himself."

Maybe I'll run away from home. Hide in a huge bushy tree. Starve the leftover me to death.

Now I am showing strangers on the street the ESSO crest above the pocket of my green shirt. I am proud to belong to ESSO, my secret club. Then I hear two adults saying I will grow out of it, all at my own pace. And I wish I didn't always remember the times I tried to keep quiet. From what I can remember, it wasn't always that way before I was born. In fact, I heard that when my real mother was pregnant with me, she patted her belly everyday and told me precisely how and when I came to be.

Wake up! Wake up! Wake! Up!

Bubbles And Ice

Five foster homes since I was seven. I've lived in five of them and I'm eleven at this time. In two days, this year's foster parents will take me to live in Newfoundland. So today I go for a skate on an enormous puddle, frozen rock hard, across the street. There I carve the letters of the loves of my life. Over and over until the blades run out of alphabet. Then I lie down in the snow.

"You all know my name and I'll never have babies," I shout at the sky, my words bouncing from sun to cloud and back again.

When I look again at the puddle I see bubbles trying to escape from the bottom of a deep frozen puddle. Bubbles with faces. Bubbles with fingers looking for someone to point to.

"You read too many comic books," my social worker says.

"So?" I say.

"So, it sounds like you live in them,"she says.

"What's so bad about that?" I ask.

"Let go. Let go of the past," she says.

The social worker walks away, her long, fancy, brown coat flapping, flapping, like long strips of bark refusing to let go of a tree.

"Just leave my bubbles alone! Do you hear me, babies? Do you hear me?" I say back and forth to the sky and puddle.

CRUTCHES

Remembrance Day. I see only the handicapped boy smelling like fresh bubble gum, face twisted with blue eyes and freckles, short straight hair the color of mahogany, legs like rubber on gymnasium wood. His crutches are gigantic knitting needles click-clacking on the quiet. Everybody in the gym looks like those kids listening to the hearts of their dogs. Listening. For pulses. Get close. Closer.

Then, the place is filled with one solemn story after another, for all those soldiers stuck in the mud of war. The man who was suddenly face-to-face with an enemy soldier looking down at him from the top of a trench but both men too shocked to shoot each other.

"I just couldn't shoot. Neither could the other guy. He looked like my cousin. Could any of you shoot your cousin? Could you?" the veteran says.

Wheel-chaired men with missing arms and legs. Men who expect us all to stand at attention. Men with honor under their skins. And only the crutch-framed boy cannot stand so easily for that one minute of trumpet playing from a cassette player. The boy stabs the floor with one of his crutches.

"Who are we talking about?" the boy says to me. "Come on, who are we talking about here?" he asks again. "And will someone, anyone, lend me your legs!"

At the front of the gym, a trumpet plays its heart out.

BECAUSE OF THE SUN'S GRACE

I refuse to believe that when I stop being afraid of one thing, I begin another fear. I see myself older, outside my house. I lean, clasping my front gate. Today's ease is being brought to me by the sun's warmth making my body temperature re-invent itself.

A father stops at my house and asks: "Would you please check to see if my son's kite is on your roof?"

"Sure, why not?" I say. I walk away from my gate. Climb off this moment. Work my way up a ladder to the roof. Find a tiny kite made of numerous sheets of brown tissue paper stretched across popsicle sticks smelling faintly of orange, of sun. The father lifts his head to me and his face looks like I had just found his lost wallet.

"Thanks for all your trouble," the father says in such a gentle voice that his words could lift the kite from my right hand to my left and my palms wouldn't know it.

The kite has survived. So have I. It's a neat trick I learned as a boy when I had both hands on my own kite string. At the time I was amazed. Had my feet apart so I could carefully measure the scooping of clouds. The plunging. My kite's briefness. Looked like my pocket turned inside-out. A heart drumming, tight above a bare hill. The sheet flap-flapping. The driving. The sky being carved into different-shaped rooms. An imaginary ladder leaning into the warmest, most spacious room. My room. Given to me by the sun's grace.

THE PRIEST, THE MOTHER

In the pew across from me, a mother and her two daughters pray themselves inside out. Pray The Virgin Mary right out of her picture frame. Pray the sandals right off St. Joseph's feet. Pray. Pray. Eyes squint in near pain. Mouths move quickly. Murmur. Murmur. Holy air. Holy breathing. One of the daughters is a deaf mute. The mother uses sign language with her. With the other girl, the mother's whispers sound like parting curtains. "I expect you both to give yourself only to God," says the shaping of her lips.

This morning's sermon moves easily from God to Allah to Buddha. As the priest talks, he is a seeing eye dog reading everyone's eyes. Some of the intense faces become more so when the priest acknowledges their zeal with an enormous smile of his own. Pious teeth. Inside the priest is probably a boy who says:

"I need your bottles and cans, parishioners. To help pay church bills."

The mother and I catch each other's eyes, as if we were born to sweat from each other's pores. Eyes that enjoy how the priest's gentle humor rescues whatever laughter was misplaced during the week. And the priest doesn't get too fancy when he says:

"God's a single higher power. If you have a problem, turn it over to that bigger power, even if at first that power is only a light bulb. If you stay inside yourself, it's like being trapped behind enemy lines. Fake it till you make it but get out of yourself."

Then the mother and I connect with each other's eyes a second time. Maybe our smiles say we are silently vowing that the priest will chart and celebrate those eye thoughts found in the involuntary muscles of people like her, like me.

"Sometimes, sins just sneak up on us," the priest says.

In a far corner of the church, an infant demonstrates a newborn sinner cry.

First Red Traffic Light

"You can't always be pleased with life as it is, Boy," the teacher preaches to me. I half-run out of the classroom. Imagine the teacher's face on display like that leftover cement bag against a wall of an aging school being made new across the street. Out in the hallway, the knuckles on my writing hand go from white to whiter. The chalk of rage. I must get out of this preaching corner I feel painted into. On the street, I search for the first red traffic light so I can walk against it and watch myself bleed. I must prove to the teacher what her classes are not doing to me, what her words say:

"Listen, Boy. Think like I think or you'll be told you have the mental agility of a pencil sharpener."

I'll never be ready for her and the way she tries to tromp around inside our heads. But she'll be proud when she realizes what I have learned about allowing the dying to take care of burying the dead, words my father gave me last week when we were out walking by a cemetery wall smelling of old flowers.

And when I find the red traffic light, there ready at the opposite corner is the teacher taking notes on how I step off the curb. After I discover why she's there, an idea runs up behind my eyes and nearly crashes right there.

How The Wolf Became A Collie

(for A.B.)

The dog does not save lives between commercials.

No, this Collie dog just sits at attention on my lawn. Forepaws highlighted in the afternoon sun, the dog imitates his ancestors by lying on its side, its back, with all four paws reaching, reaching for ornaments of sun. His front and back halves look like they once belonged to different animals. It's this imperfection that makes the dog so gold, so beautiful. His ancestors planned it. They passed on only their best parts. In another skin, another time, the Collie was a wolf with clipped claws, filed teeth, and an appearance that never took advantage of another animal. The dog didn't belong to the pack. He always smelled like an almost clean dog and nothing else. Never fought for territory. Only barked at the moon occasionally on clear nights, as if the moon were a gold ball the Collie wanted but could not reach. Ever so gradually, the wolf became the Collie it always wanted to be.

Today, its bark forces real wolves to scratch their ears. Makes them think for the first time about how their own growls began.

This dog does not save lives.

GINA

(for B.G.)

I know why Gina pretends to be her stuffed green dog. I know why she aims her eyes straight at me on this morning of cool sun. Gina still has that newborn smell and her laugh is a handful of warm water on my face after a close shave. Perhaps, she waits for the world to get better. Waits for the wound to heal between the two halves inside my head.

"Nobody should have your pain," Gina's eyes seem to say.

And in her left hand, Gina holds a head of cheek-bursting humor and simple, imaginary questions such as:

"Do you like my dog?"

This is Gina's way of taking me to those clear, clear places, the centers of her eyes. In her right hand, Gina grasps something to pass on to me. Something I will learn today. Face to face with her.

Then Gina and I step outside, forgetting the stuffed dog. I feel her almost kissing life into my neck, my face. The clean, sure breathing of a child. Placing her gently on the grass, I wait for the lesson to begin. The time for me to be teachable is now. And part of the toy dog is still here, staring through Gina with the plainness of love.

CLEARASIL CHINS

At the time I had just a dab of Clearasil on my chin. She had a close place next to my skin when I was fifteen. My arms wrapped around her in the dark. Our lips mashed together. Clearasil-caked chins grinding together, chin on chin. The taste of her chalky chin, the taste of still-wet cement, made my stomach do handstands. I wanted her stomach to taste my chin like it never had before. Now she and I are seated next to each other on an airplane heading to Montreal, and when I recognize her, I think Clearasil, chins, lips, and tongues.

She says she remembers me but I can tell she's not quite sure. Or perhaps the scars have scabbed her memory for good.

"I've recently become a medical doctor at the University of Calgary in pediatrics," she says. "Did I ever tell you that I hated being a kid?" she adds. "

"No. Not that I remember," I say.

I don't bring up the Clearasil incident. The woman is flying back to Montreal to be with her husband who runs a hardware store. She adores the integrity of her man. I glance discreetly at her present chin. Still bumpy. Still scarred. Still covered.

"After you tell me why you want to fix kids, I'm all yours," I say half-jokingly.

The aircraft's lights dim and the movie begins.

PRETENDING TO BE DEAD

I pretend to be dead. For the first time I lie on my back, the coarse grass like tiny arrows in my spine. On my chest, a black dog hesitates. Licks. Hesitates. Licks my face. As if it wants to know why I'm pretending to die.

Then I see myself walking by with a bag of groceries in one arm. The bag contains dried figs, raisins, dried apricots, unblanched almonds, dried prunes, dried bananas, Bran Flakes and All-Bran — all for a cereal I make. When I stop to watch the dog and the lying-down-me more closely, I realize my death game needs rules, like you can live more than once. After, I lift my laughing head, like a huge insect, right out of the grass. There are sudden pedestrians walking by but the standing-up-me is gone I used to be a grasshopper in another life and any grass would do. Dying. The joy of dying, like the burst of fresh bubble gum, filling my mouth.

In one way, I am more ready to die now because today, all is plate glass: there are no waves crashing onto a beach, no storms. The insanity of melodramas. In another way, I want to live until clocks invent new numbers. Recently, I have been learning how to breathe again, the knot in my stomach slowly unraveling, as if the knot were just another waste product. I pretend to eat better. No booze. No cigarettes. Exercise. Daily meditation. Vitamin pills. I think about the Hungarian condom containing a computer chip that plays the Internationale "Arise ye workers!". Still looking for heart. Remembering the newspaper cartoon showing an enormous convention hall for Normal Anonymous convention delegates containing only three people. For now I have no strings attached to me or to the brown-bagged nourishment in my arms. But there's a second time for anything, here lying on the carnal teeth of grass.

Am I standing or lying down?

Will I take the bridge instead of the water?

SEEING DEATH PERFORM LIKE IT DOES
(for "Boraino")

You weave a slow-motion shuffle around the white silk nest that is your mother's coffin. With small, dipping motions, you check to make sure her chocolate-colored teddy bear is tucked in, eyes facing your mother's, like a fur angel. And right after that, all the mothering she ever gave you becomes trapped in your throat, like wet leaves in a drain pipe. Cry! Cry, Boraino! Please cry! And you do. You do. After, you barely kiss your mother's forehead in case a tear might awaken her before she reaches the other side of now. Fear not, Boraino! She has already tasted your heart salt and has memorized the story of your skin. And your mother lays there, hair coiffed in cloud-white curls, as if the curls were handfuls of snowflakes never to melt. You know, Boriano - like you, who never preaches but just speaks and the twisted U-turns in our brains suddenly straighten out! Maybe, your mother is just resting there in her death dress because right above her is a floating heart the size of her coffin. And mourners each place a finger on a heart wall hoping to finger-dance with her pulse one last time. Vitality. Here in this ornate storybook church. Vitality. Here in this place of walls and walls of freshly-painted icons speaking new into the old Ukraine.

The woman beside me lets her head slip to her chest, her neck straining with the weight of it all. Then she lifts her face through the persistent sunlight and moves her prayer lips, as if a ventriloquist has a hand in all of this. Seeing Death perform like it does makes her eyes water up, as if they were miniature measuring cups. And when my own eyes join hers, we are at the top of a dam which is as high as a cloud and peering down into a valley filled with reasons why love is the opposite of fear. The woman's fingers are clean, clear, no nail polish or rings and scrubbed to the truth of her bone. I watch her fingers, like new chalk pieces, shape letters, then words, to help define the underside of joy. Fingers that have been aired out just enough, on her walk to church. Fingers light enough to trace, then caress the awful beauty of your aching, Boraino.

Later, I watch you slide back to where your family sits, and your tall replica of humanity drops into place, your tears carving pathways through sunlight particles. Finally, you are on your feet again and gliding towards that hovering heart. You touch the heart with one finger, two fingers... and your touching... your touching is so delicate, Boraino, your fingerprints leave you forever and I hear both you and your mother sigh...at exactly the same time.

II
NOT IN MY OWN SKIN

Color

"I cannot live in my own skin," I say to myself in the bathroom mirror. "And what's so special about your skin?" the face says back to me.

"Just can't separate myself from Native People and how they blend into the elements," I say to the face.

"What's that supposed to mean?" the face asks.

"I want a gift. My sleep seizure guardian. I want my sleep back," I say, as if sleep were something I lost, like a credit card.

Why I am suddenly concerned for the colors of red and white, is baffling. Although I'm nearly as white as chalk, maybe I'm really a Native leader whose skin is the same color as a river on fire. All this for sleep.

Today at noon, on the prairie, when I stand at a certain place, the sky rises like a teepee to the highest point of a rainbow. I see myself refusing all food in order to find a ...vision, an answer for my starving people. If need be, I will wait until dusk. Then I'll become an island of possibilities in the sunset's palm.

Later, I will shut my eyes and hunt for sleep, even if I have to scoop the moon out of the sky and swallow it, like a pill.

NAME

I have to do something. Another man with the same name as me owes money from Pole to Pole. Now I receive phone calls from collection agencies:

"You owe three hundred dollars on your computer. You still haven't paid your bill for two hundred dollars worth of clothes. It's either pay or see you in court or go to jail."

Yesterday, after a sheriff showed up at my door, I obtained an unlisted telephone number. However, I plan no revenge for the other man. In fact, on the flip side of my impatience is a curiosity to meet this other man. Let him open his heart and his head. Discuss how our names were chosen. Laugh at my ironic frugality. But if our meeting becomes focused on some hidden anger because of my phone book absence, then the get-together could kill us both. And I may tell the other man exactly how I feel about this crazy duality. The mistakes. The fear. The threats to my skin. I hope to ask the other man to take our name to a faraway city. Leave it there. Return as a different me.

Outside, I see a leaf turn its spine to the sun and its veins are my initials.

Mole Removal

This morning my neighbor had it removed. It is the only mole of its kind. Now there is the smell of gunpowder escaping from his facial wound.

"What about that smell?" I ask him.

"Maybe it's just wind blowing the wrong way," he says. The smell causes my neighbor to question himself for the first time ever in my presence: "At least I think that's what it is," he says.

The aimless wind he speaks of is comprised of leftovers from when he last lost his temper yesterday when someone said:

"From a distance, your mole looks like a bullet hole."

"WHAT'S THAT SUPPOSED TO MEAN?' he yelled.

Today, uncovered, the neighbor realizes that his face stinks. A medical marvel. No blood. Just his own mix of explosives.

The neighbor used to eliminate anyone who dared to question his frequent outbursts of impatience:

"I'm right. Got it," he'd say, his teeth grinding the yellow off each other.

He thought he'd have the mole removed for health reasons. Yet, the real reason may have something to do with last Friday night when my neighbor and I went to a spiritualist meeting at a downtown chapel to see if my neighbor could contact the spirit of his dead brother. The medium told my neighbor:

"Whenever you wear that yellow sweater of yours, you allow everyone to push you around. And if you don't believe me, ask your brother."

Grabbing onto his sweater sleeves, as if they were the straps of a life jacket, my neighbor replied:

"No wonder I'm so overwhelmed by myself."

Then I hear a gun being cocked. Hear silence too.

CARTOON

Ned's face once belonged to an eager and honest mind. That was until he was able to push people away on a regular basis. All because his mother could not keep her hands off him. He'd walk by her in the kitchen or hallway and she'd grab him by the face, then kiss and hug him until she emptied her desires.

"The only person I can cuddle with is my wife, Beverly. My kids are on their own," Ned told me last week.

When he walks down the hallway at work, his hair, the color of an aluminum pie plate, hangs over his forehead, as if it were hanging on to his boyhood. The rest of him is an over-stuffed toad waddling, like a resident wisdom king. Motherhen soothsayer of the workplace. Deadened by, but the omniscient buddha of, stress.

"My wife tells me that if I become less stressed than I am now, I'd fall asleep," he proclaimed last week.

Now his face is a protected face and its mouth is shut tightly, its nose hard. The cosmetics of Ned's face are as rough as a poorly-plastered wall, an uneasy curiosity for passers-by. If it were an in-between face, Ned's face would not be noticed. Readers might realize that his face bends and twists because it grows with his duties as a reporter of sorts. Ned can't stop his looking. He cannot eliminate his hearing. Ned's face is attached to an "arm's length" world. And what is an in-between face? It is the face of a huge, friendly mammal. On top of the mammal's head, a mouse skitters back and forth like a safe new idea above Ned's eyes.

FURNACE

Flowers sometimes scare my boss. They smell sweet but they are not always obvious and that makes them dangerous to him.

"I believe only what I feel. Not what I see or smell," he tells me. "Sometimes I think the petals only exist to beat me to death with the sweetness of their smells, their shapes," he told me not long ago.

"I have two furnaces at home for good reason," the boss says. "I need to feel the heat right next to my January skin. Remember, I am the father of four young daughters. I've always wanted a son to carry both myself and my hockey stick more upright. So the four girls often pretend to be hockey players, keeping their heads up and their rear-ends in whenever they cross my blueline. And the girls never ever mention the word 'FLOWER' when I'm around."

Last month at a staff party, the boss' wife gave him such a stern look, it seemed as if she were locking up his testicles in a jar of vinegar for the night. But when his wife stopped paying attention, the boss measured another wife with her clothes off. Looked her up and down. Up and down. His eyes peeling back the fabric of his desire:

"Wonder what she's like with her clothes off?" he snickers after gulping down his rye and water.

"That's my wife. I'll go tell her you asked," I say.

"No! Don't do that. Sorry."

"Sure. Why not? She'll get a kick out of it."

When I tell my wife, she says nothing and grits her teeth until they are smeared with lipstick. And when my boss comes over to apologize, my wife asks him:

"Is there a hole in the ceiling?"

As my boss looks up, she kicks him so hard that his ears are now wearing testicles as earrings.

"I love your earrings," my wife says. "Did your wife lend them to you?"

In another corner of the room, still another woman is his boss. His eyes stay only on hers when she's one of the boys. Unless, of course, that boss woman wants to know the quickest and the most flowerless way to his heart.

"And if she aims for my stomach, she's aiming too high," the boss loudly whispers into a man's ear next to me, his voice desperate and smelling like a dead rose, even from a short distance.

The cognac in my cut glass is now warm enough.

In This Town Of Crepe Paper Sun

In The Copper Cup Cafe, skillets and plastic flowers are synthetic bird nests glued to the walls. A mother-and-daughter waitress team offer pliable menus and speak occasional French together.

"Plus vite! Plus vite! Faster! Faster!" they say to each other. "Lots of customers."

The restaurant walls know their voices so well. Tin foil decorative frying pans listen like two ears.

I sit by myself in my booth in the comfort of cigarette smoke, as if I were filling the booth with a cloud brought inside. I overfill my space with smoke before supper to ensure quiet time as I select my meal.

When I finally do order, I remind the mother waitress: "You're lucky this café serves only hearty food, or the place would go belly-up in this town of crepe paper sun."

The waitress moves closer.

"What do you mean by 'crepe paper sun'?" she asks, her accent as thick as pancake syrup.

Then I point to her head, my own head, read her thinking, and gesture outside to the perpetually hazy sky, the color of ash.

"Regarde," I say. "Regarde! See! See!"

Plates rattle. The smells of many suppers. She knows the answer better than I do because of her own name for sky.

ROAD

As I drive over the old road, I unbutton my shirt and ask myself if the car is on fire. The sun is outdoing itself as I continue driving. I want to keep up with the sunset which is the best part of my day. On the radio, a baseball game allows me to pretend I'm there watching the electronic scoreboard and nudging spectators about the cartooned ballplayers:

"Watch the second-baseman. Look for a steal," I yell.

Outside the vehicle, road sign arrows sharpen themselves in the sun and on the quickness of my passing. And that makes me feel like the person who invented the joy of a perfect game. The smell of peanuts, popcorn. The crack of a bat. The ball smacking against the catcher's mitt. The organ's music following a foul ball. The crowd's sudden cheers, jeers. Once upon a time, I was too hard on myself, like the player who just struck out, his bottom lip dragging on the turf back to the dugout. Dugouts.

"I've had it rough. All my bats have holes in them!" I'd say.

I pray I will not go back to that time when I worried about non-existent suitcases slipping off the roof of my car whenever I went anywhere, even though I hadn't had a vacation in years. Dug. Outs.

In my hands, I feel the smoothness of a brand new bat. Smell the hickory. My turn.

The sun waits for me on the other side of center field.

THE SHAPES ARE GENTLE QUESTIONS

The shapes sticking out near the water are not the usual mother and father trees.

The shapes are gentle questions.

"Is the water clean enough to drink?" they seem to ask me.

"Are you feeling better?"

In the trees, there are no birds or leaves. The branches hold leftover notes of a sad piano song I can still hear. Heat radiating from the soil comes from an invisible sun, a sun that may be more useful in the earth's core, like an overused spotlight from the night before. I am by myself at the keys of this beauty. Perhaps, the tree branches are more intrigued with the pain of my singing, the sorrow that will not leave. That could explain why I leave my piano bench and stroll to the lip of the water. Curious. There I suck in as much oxygen as possible. When I return to my piano bench relieved, my new ballad clearly promises that I should be ready for more questions. Soon.

Above, a crow as black as a wolf's mouth, sings the same answer over and over.

WINNING TREES

I am dwarfed. In a meadow, I wait under the immensity of two cypress trees near a swamp and inhale the dampness. The first tree grows downward through the mirk. It aims for the earth's center. The second tree races up through the sky. Cattails wait to applaud. Who will brush the sun or the earth's core first?

The first tree was once the spear of a prehistoric hunter. The hunter caught nothing to eat so he flung his rage back into the ground, as if the earth were a vengeful supermarket. The anger became a tree. And the tree got in the last word.

At the base of the second tree leans a ladder once belonging to a foolish reporter who insisted on climbing alone into a world where behavior is not controlled by words. The reporter never made it back. But before he left, he tried to teach me all he knew.

"If you don't have stamina, you're nothing as a writer," he said.

As I await the winner, I hear birds sing about seeds that have not yet sprouted.

THAT BRIGHT OR THAT DARK

I want what I deserve.

Wearing clear-cut bifocals, I cross my arms like two birch logs, my flannel work shirt buttoned to my chin.

"I dare you!" I say. "I dare you!" I scowl at the clock.

I will outwait the clock above my head. I cross and re-cross my legs waiting for my paycheque to be replaced. For some reasonJreceivedonly half my usual pay this week.

"It may be a computer error but they'd better straighten it out!" I say loud enough for everyone to hear. At my elbow on a table, is a blooming cactus plant. The heat the cactus needs radiates from me. Black pools under my eyes urge the cactus to flower, even in the fading vanilla light of this outer office.

"I'd love to make a singer out of the first screaming employee to touch that cactus," I say at no one in particular.

Behind me, I feel the afternoon sun leaving my shoulders. Hot water becoming warm. I have nearly filled this room with skins that simply won't fit. If there were a fireplace here, I could fill it with enough wood to make a steam engine go for hours.

My determination is that bright or that dark.

SCRATCHING ON HIS CRANIUM

(in memory of C.E.)

The balding, sloped-shouldered man has ten months to live and he surrounds himself with his illness.

His wife crosses off each day of the calendar, as if she were performing surgery. She asks:

"What are you thinking about now that this malignant growth will soon spurt into your brain?"

"At least doctors won't be grinding into my skull anymore," Jay laughs, as if his brain no longer had any use for sentiment.

In his early forties, he still has lots of boy in him but the scratching on Jay's cranium is becoming too noisy.

"I can't believe how many times those so-called 'medical experts' have shaken their own heads about you," his wife says.

And the right side of Jay's brain won't allow him to build a barrier for his garbage cans in his backyard. Instead, he nails everything flat to the ground. Meanwhile, the man's wife takes pills from sunrise to sunrise and is addicted to prayer.

"Please give my husband, Jay his thoughts back. Please!" she begs the statues in her bedroom and church.

Yesterday, she nearly phoned a handyman to build that garbage can barrier because dogs and cats were helping themselves to their garbage, as if a nearly-dead man's leftovers had a special taste. A smell.

Right now Jay's wife observes him trying to stuff a spring back into a digital pen.

"Ink will never give you the proper time," she teases.

Jay doesn't laugh because he read a book last week that gave him hope after shedding the skins of pain. He also discovered how time never returns to a watch or clock but he will take his digital pen with him anyway.

Then, quite suddenly, Jay loses his speech, as if he were poking fun at himself. When just as abruptly his speech returns, Jay presents himself with an imaginary award:

"Congratulations, Jay, you are the winner of this very special digital pen. Take it wherever you go. It's waterproof. Fireproof. Shockproof."

Then Jay falls backwards onto the sofa right next to his wife.

"My left hand cannot type and my right hand is just too tired," he says.

"I'll be your pen," his wife says.

Jay leaps to his feet. Grabs a newspaper. Folds it three times. Tries to swat a huge moth circling the hallway light. Lunges at the walls making his shadows swell in the light. The moth escapes. Jay smacks the insect's wall-to-wall shadow.

Finally, he says: "Doctors don't want to leave me as that neighborhood man who mothers warn their kids about. My skull grows weary. From the eyes of children. From my own words?"

In an insect world, Jay would be left alone.

Sixty Then Ninety

(for A.E.G.)

I still hear my father-in-law in my house, although he's been dead for three years. His constant advice is as insistent as autumn breathing:

"Why don't you write a good detective story like Columbo or something. Columbo is very, very, very good!"

Now I use my father-in-law's old mustache kit— wax, brush, and tiny comb.

"Keep order on the top lip," he often joked.

Used to kid me about carrying his coffin. But my father-in-law's cockiness in the eye of death surfaced whenever I asked him if it were too late for him to stop smoking. Now I see each mustache hair as a secret, like a treaty my father-in-law once signed with me that the world is really a detective story. Chances are he's still puffing in his grave. When the rest of the family is buried beside him, they will become a heap of lemons squeezed dry of all bitterness. And I will celebrate, with the strongest portion of my own heart, the day my father-in-law's counselling ends.

I cannot forget his last cigarette, burning only hours before his sixty-year-old body, looking ninety, was lowered into a hurriedly dug grave of uneasy worms. And all this after-death sentiment turns me into a child trying to do handstands across a kitchen floor covered with molasses. Father-in-law molasses.

I listen for the WHOOSH of his next match.

III
REPORTER

LEPERS

The grey-haired leper drenched in aftershave, points to a graveyard and emphasizes miles and miles of beach. Gestures to trees planted as a shield. Trees nurtured by real leper bones shortly after this colony began. When I offer a handshake and my name, the leper says:

"Do you know what you're doing, Sir? Is your hand part of you? Let me remind you that if my medication ever stopped, these contagious sores would flash themselves at the sun and crawl through the pores of your hands, like starving insects."

Since he was left on this island at seventeen, the leper loves joking about various parts of his body falling to the ground, like dead leaves, scaring the sunglasses off tourist faces. Now, at fifty-seven, he laughs longest at his non-leper sisters, keeping a safe distance, living in faraway New York City. These are the same sisters who remind him yearly that they mean well in their Christmas cards.

Then the leper brings me to the only restaurant-general store on this island. In the store, there is a 1905 photograph of a group of happy lepers, a piano, a broken black and white television in a corner with an unknown thriving plant on top, and other leper clerks who can't do enough for me.

(This story wants to end itself but doesn't know how to do it.)

Finally the leper says to me: "I normally just like being an anonymous clerk putting in an honest day's work. But not today. Why don't we just celebrate the touching of hands? Would you like to hear my wife play CARNIVAL TIME on the piano? Pretend... pretend you're at a circus!"

From A Holy Roman Skull Factory

Halfway through the first showing of his paintings, the artist gathers a small group of admirers around him and speaks with pride about his stay in a mental hospital, or as he calls it: A Holy Roman Skull Factory. Isolated. Medicated. Frozen. Shocked. Even had the nerves on his forehead severed. And he was just fired from his Communications Officer job at The Human Rights Commission. Diagnosed as a schizophrenic. Recently self-published his own novel called FAR FROM FEELING PITY. Wrote poems that were so introverted they sounded like tacks pouring one by one, two by two, three by three... onto a cement floor. Smoked two packs of Export A's a day. Wore black, long-sleeved shirts and the same pair of blue jeans day after day. And last month in the hospital, he was forced to have his jeans washed for the first time ever. The clean feeling nearly killed him.

Tonight, the artist's rage shows itself when he talks of discovering how his wife was sleeping with his psychiatrist at the time. The reporter in me asks the artist:

"How could you possibly allow the same man to enter your head and wife at the same time and tell everyone about it?"

The artist responds by smashing one of his best works against a wall and then calmly stating:

"That... is none of your business."

Outside, in the still summer night, a child bounces a ball, back and forth, back and forth.

WHISKEY ON WHITE

Ernie and his shaking must be at least sixty years of age.

"I'm hopeful about everything in life," he says to me, his voice moving up and down , as if someone else were controlling the volume.

When he opens his suitcase, a white shirt still unwrapped stares back at me. A bleached headstone. Around the white shirt, a dozen mickeys of whiskey lay on their backs. Ernie opens a bottle. Apologizes for having the flu. A hangover. And while he quickly combs his hair, bits of blood remain in his comb and crumble to his shoulders, like red dandruff, as if he had just raked all the pain from his head. Afterwards, Ernie holds up his microphone comb. Speaks like an FM radio announcer:

"I'd like to brush up on my broadcasting skills. Get a job with the CBC. Maybe, some obscure HOCKEY NIGHT IN CANADA position. Work at the far end of the darkest corridor. Emerge only to collect my paycheque."

"What about hockey?" I ask. "I hear you love it."

"I live it," Ernie answers.

Ernie's stick protected a skinny boyhood. Now, he stands in his freshly laundered shirt, a mickey in one hand and a fantasy hockey stick in the other. I imagine Ernie at center ice. I see him leaning just enough on his stick.The blue and red lines do not waver. I watch him deke his way around his shaking.

Then he says:

"Some say I have an allergy to booze and I seem to breaking out in spots such as: Calgary, Montreal, Chicago, Reno and Halifax."

There is something bloody here, here and here.

43

Except For Bees

He's never had an affair, except with bees. As a boy, the priest lay on his belly for hours and studied bees flying back and forth from their honeycombs; this was the only time he forgot his shyness.

As a man, the priest has heard so many stories about addictions in his sin-listing job that he's forgotten what the word 'shy' means.

"I got hooked on the drowning of bees and their honey a long time ago," the priest tells me.

Then he holds up a chunk from his latest honeycomb and the word 'honey' sounds like it is glued to a wall of the priest's heart.

"This is the first time I've been able to tell anyone about my problem," he says to me. "No more denial. It all started with my favorite aunt who once drowned two pieces of toast for me in honey. I ate six more honey-drenched pieces of toast that morning. It hasn't stopped since."

Today, the priest raises bees behind the church to keep his honey fresh and steady.

Then the priest asks:

"Would all this have anything to do with my being in a California encounter group last year? When the sessions ended, the leader told me I was so screwed up because I'm a priest!"

After the priest grabs the huge chunk of honey he is about to give me, he holds it up to the lights and asks

"Can being screwed up have anything to do with honey or bees? Let's go outside and look."

In the priest's backyard, we study each and every flower but their faces only smile.

PIRATES AND MORONS

"I'm fifty years old today," Steven yells into my reporter's ear, and I jump back, as if the yelling had just bored a hole straight through to the other side of my head.

Steven's hair is the same silver gray as a beer can and he has just a thimbleful of beard on his chin. The sad violin of his talking surprises me and his shoulders droop so naturally, I wonder if he surrendered to life before he took his first breath.

Apparently, Steven lost one eyeball in a table saw accident. A black patch covers the hole.

"I never feel like that moron pirate the police say I am," he says.

Because of a second accident at his workbench with the head of a nail scraping his eyeball, his other eye is eighty percent blind.

"The cops told me last time that I'd be safer on the high seas," he says.

In 1985, Steven committed armed robbery when he still had one good eye. Lately, he's been shoplifting only. Robberies are too much work. Steven's lawyer says that his crimes are unusual because theft is normally committed by younger crooks. The lawyer will plead guilty to more obvious charges. Maybe lessen the sentence.

Steven's only remorse is doing any time at all. Prison has done nothing to change him. And stealing helps him bring order to his life. In jail he can't steal very much. Steven cannot read. Or write. Soon he will again misread directions and have another accident. Then, he'll be readmitted into the prison hospital.

Steven's face tightens, like his stomach did the first time he showered in jail. "I want out of this crook business. I can no longer tell if anyone is watching while I commit a crime," he says.

When I chuckle, Steven hears other laughter from those real pirates at the bottom of their rich graves, authentic pirates who never thought of quitting.

Steven's words are not safe. Even in my own ear.

FAST ONES

Time to pull a fast one. The male office workers in this building supply company all arrive at work dressed as construction workers and become real men for their women co-workers. None of the men have showered or shaved but the women found out beforehand and planned a joke of their own. They come to work as real women, wearing gingham dresses and bonnets, smelling like fresh daisies. And they announce:

"We will most certainly cook and serve lunch to our men!"

At noon, the men trudge into the lunchroom. Look as manly as possible by scratching their faces, chests and crotches. Pete wears a construction helmet and grunts harder than the others. He wears his weekend clothes: faded jeans, steel-toed construction boots, a half-dirty T-shirt. He carries a dented, steel lunch bucket with an uncut all-meat sandwich. Tells what he considers MEN ONLY jokes:

"Hey guys, it's Women's Lib. Week. Take a Broad out to lunch and make her pay".

In his real life, Pete lifts weights and gulps vitamins daily. On most workdays, Pete is heard snickering about what he'd like to do with a couple of the women on staff. But Pete is at a loss right now. The more he tries his real man routine, the quieter the other male staff members become. Meanwhile, the real women in the gingham dresses are puzzled and their daisy-fresh smell fades. They serve him his lunch, as if nobody were seated in his chair. Pete is not his usual self. I see Pete as that piece of land which suddenly discovers its trees are quotation marks around its natural habits.

Pete puffs on a cigar as if he were rehearsing for a hernia.

"Gimme a match will ya," he says. "Come on Honey, ANY-BODY, light me up, will ya! The joke's over!"

The microwave oven rings three times and a male co-worker says:

"It's okay, Pete."

"What's okay? asks Pete.

"We all know," says the co-worker.

"Know what?"

"That maybe you spent too much time pumping."

"Pumping what?"

"Iron. Inside your mother's womb."

BINGO AND SEX

Shortly after his leg is placed in a cast, Sam finds out his wife is more interested in Bingo than sex. Yet her climaxes are more frequent, more consistent. And all this is dumped on my table before Sam parks himself in a chair and orders a beer.

And only two weeks ago, Sam tried to catch another workmate who fell from three stories up.

"He got away with a bruised back but I broke my leg," says Sam. " After, I tried buying my wife sheer green underwear because I thought she'd appreciate that I remembered green was her favorite color."

Still, Sam's wife is leaving him.

"She's got herself a Bingo boyfriend now, so I don't have a chance," he says.

At my table, Sam smokes faster. Talks louder.

"More beer!" he orders. His knuckles change colors like traffic lights. He clenches his empty glass and nearly wears himself out doing it.

"All of that great sex I had with her, well... I never knew. She faked it so well. Even joked in bed. 'Under the B, me,' she used to say. Guess I never knew the real numbers on her card. WAITER, another round, please."

Sam will find out tomorrow what his prize is when he awakens with the smells of beer and cigarettes still on his nostrils.

MUSIC RECITAL

A man with a half helmet of leather springs from his wheelchair at the music recital. Then he pops a cassette into the portable under his seat and disco-dances wildly in the aisle. Causes the audience to squirm behind its complexions.

"People are here for a formal recital, not spontaneity," a mother says to me.

The crowd threatens to burst from throat-clearing. Makes the hand clapping become an on-again, off-again rain. The music stops. His dancing doesn't. The clapping peters out like the last raindrops from a gutter.

Just one person applauds for the wheelchair man now. She too is in a wheelchair and encourages the half-helmeted man to steal the show.

"I'll wait until he has completely taken the evening away from everyone and then I'll ask someone to ease him back into his wheelchair," says the wheel-chaired woman to anyone who will listen.

In the air, the smell of coffee and doughnuts and the sounds of feet shuffling punctuate the room. Throats are cleared. Legs cross and re-cross each other. Programs are folded, curled, from one hand to the next.

Even I want to roll him out the back exit so the audience doesn't have to witness how long the wheelchair man's posture can remain in his frozen bow.

"Look! Listen! I'm all me!" the wheelchair man shouts.

A woman in her sixties plumps herself down on his knees and plays her accordion, like a heart unfolding.

TIMING

Sometimes the psychologist likes to work outside heads. In front of the funeral home, the psychologist says to me:

"Know something, I'm finally released from my father's Christmas Day death more than thirty years ago. But my mother had to die to do it."

Then the psychologist forgives himself for yelling at his mother on her deathbed:

"I had to do it, Mom! You drove me crazy every time you opened your mouth about anything."

Waiting nearby is the psychologist's brother-in-law who whispers to me:

"Don't take him seriously because he tends to dramatize experiences. Remember, he's a psychologist."

Once the two men had visited the Columbia Icefields together and the brother-in-law simply saw a river of ice. The psychologist saw stories of bodies being lost forever between walls of ice. Heard heroes clinging to icy lips, begging, begging, their words glacier-deadened. Configurations of a slow, perfect passing. The fantastic shaping of screams. And I also know that the brother-in-law's most stimulating moments are visits to new shopping malls. So I see a story of one man looking for bargains while the other suffers torment, watching, waiting... almost celebrating pain. The psychologist is his own hero. He thinks shopping-center death. Feels his heart trying to make sense of its walls, the red emotional handcuffing.

I go for a ride with the psychologist. In the car, his window is rolled down completely. His nerves unravel like the thread on a never-ending spool. Each time he accelerates, the psychologist babbles about the pain of something or other.

"What advice would a psychologist give himself at a time such as this?" I ask.

He answers by snapping his wrist at the passing wind, crushing his mother's 'IN MEMORY OF' card and flinging thirty years out the car window. I watch the card blow right back in his face like a startled, legless moth.

51

BETTY ANN PICKS A CARD
(for S.)

Betty Ann has a face that moves like it is covered in plastic wrap and it makes the reporter in me laugh. She says she can speak of the child that is her and the child that is not her. Only one at a time.

"This was caused by my father's gambling under the Jacques Cartier Bridge, the one place that was off limits to the Montreal police," she says.

"What do you mean?" I ask.

"My father lived his life as a secret," she says. "He had no Social Insurance Number, as if he loved the idea of not existing for the government. No Medicare. Took taxis everywhere. Did time in jail once when the police broke up an illegal game in the back room of a bakery. And no bedtime stories for me. Mother had to hide the rent money. His livelihood was a calendar of card games. I made up stories when the school asked what my father did for a living: Bus driver. Accountant. Manager. Clerk. A company I never remembered. Holidays were when my father felt the odds were so poor, he remained glued to his chair, his face buried in a National Geographic magazine stolen from the library. Often he would be home at odd times of the day and I'd be shocked to find him there, his black-haired, mole-like head never explaining why. And always he wore a long-sleeved white shirt, no tie and black slacks."

One Sunday morning, Betty Ann's mother had accidentally locked herself outside their apartment, dressed only in a nightgown. To get a key, her mother flagged down a taxi and rode all the way to the Jacques Cartier Bridge. When the father saw his wife like that, he almost gave up cards forever. Nearly wasn't enough for Betty Ann; she was running out of make-believe answers.

Betty Ann recalls tugging her father's pant leg. Tugging for him to help her with her puzzle.

"Go play downstairs, Darling," he'd say every time.

Occasionally, her father looked down at her in the yard, his pant legs rolled up on a late summer afternoon and planning that evening's card game.

Even though her father has been dead for seven years, Betty Ann still practices asking him what he sees in her.

A family photograph on the wall responds.

HANGING AS A DROPLET OF RAIN

In the sunny mirrors of the girl's eyes, I notice the remains of her house, crushed into the ground only an hour ago by wind. And the storm still brews, the air smelling like damp clothes. The girl's smile is a thick rubber band and it will not let go of her face. Odd strands of hair seem to divide her eyes, her aching. Hanging from a shoulder, her dress looks as if it has had the colors whipped out of it. And her partially closed mouth looks like it has been violated and prepares to fall off her face.

"Only feel sorry for the lost and homeless was what the nuns taught me in school," she says to me. "Never ever for myself. Last week, a nun spread thick cocoa and water over my face because I have such black hair. She made me visit every class-room so everyone would feel more sorry for all the poor African children and give more of our pennies. Took me days to wash out all the chocolate."

This makes me see the girl's photograph hanging as a droplet of rain from the last tree branch in front of where her home once was. Makes me hear the girl's teacher.

I listen to the chocolate drums.

Temperature

Men trade their sex stories. At a nearby table I overhear a freight truck driver say to the room:

"I'll bet women talk far more about sex than men do."

Apparently, the going price is at least two hundred dollars for top pleasure in Winnipeg, Calgary and Vancouver. One of the long-distance drivers, who is as tall as he is wide, tells the longest story:

"You should've seen the woman I had. We did it so often that I bleached her forehead."

Then the same driver confirms that his own sexual hunger is always satisfied on the road. Afterwards, the driver turns up his jean cuff to use as an ashtray, as if the cuff were a trophy of sorts.

At the next table I laugh hardest when someone points to the long-distance driver's jean cuff and warns:

"Be careful! Your pants could catch fire and you'll never be able to have sex again."

When the laughter is gradually replaced with the usual bar chatter, I think of the driver's words as one continuous but progressively weaker sunset after another and the reason women talk more about sex is that they probably think about it more often than he ever could.

Outside, the rain falls like measured sperm.

CREE MOMENT

In a tavern reeking of beer, smoke and vomit, the Cree demands:

"You a social worker or something?"

I laugh so hard I nearly smash my half-fists through the table-top. Then the Cree points to another white man with long black hair and dressed in a buckskin jacket. After, the Cree glares at the buckskin white man and says:

"See that social worker over there? Well, he's driving me nuts. He worries too much about me."

"Come on over here and have a non-social worker beer with me," I offer.

At my table, the Cree says little, no matter how much I try to strike up a conversation. And soon a staring match develops between the Cree and the social worker. Free beer for the Cree and me. Courtesy of the social worker. The more beer sent to our table, the more the Cree calls the social worker HONKEY. The more I nearly choke on my own laughter, the more the Cree says:

"Now repeat after me: HONKEY, HONKEY, HONKEY."

I imagine the free beer flowing our way forever and I smile at the social worker after each round.

"How much pounding will it take to wear down that social worker's buck skinned, black-haired heart," I mutter to myself. A well-intentioned heart that will soon be dragging its arteries, like tired road signs, on the tavern floor.

Soon, someone will have to mop up.

CRAYONS

Sex. I'm told that Canadians are obsessed with sex and the words are stabbing my quiet. Two Irishmen at the next table say I must answer to Canada's preoccupation with sex.

"Back in Ireland, sex is kept in bedrooms, not up on billboards," the two men insist.

"Yes, I am Canadian, and yes, I love sex. Lots of it. Don't you?" I say.

"No. And don't tell us to go back to Ireland if we don't like it here," the two men yell, like a pair of short-circuiting stereo speakers.

"I wouldn't dream of ordering you guys to drink up and go back to Ireland, to the private of your parts. Never. It's not me."

"What do you mean by 'parts'?" one of them asks.

My ears suddenly stop functioning. These two men make me curious but I don't want their voices.

A waiter overhears. "You two should go and see the steamy porno flick next door. In case. Just in case," he says.

"In case what?" the older of the two men demand.

"In case you never have sex again," the waiter says.

The waiter and I eye each other, like two boys in the middle of a life-long prank. We casually wait for the Irish response. Nothing. Instead, the two Irishmen mutter. Curse. Mutter again. Run fingers up and down their beer glasses. Slide rings up and down their fingers, as if peeling the wrappings from wax crayons.

The tavern door opens abruptly to a black eye of night.

SMOKE AND ANGEL HAIR

The woman with a scar running down her cheek like an upper case 'J', does not like me looking at her on the park bench and gives me an eye as cold as a new ice cube. She is wrapped in a brown tweed winter coat; a red kerchief is knotted under her chin. Sucking so deeply on her cigarette, she threatens to turn herself inside-out. I swear I hear her brain preparing for me, as if it were a chalkboard being swished clean. She exhales. Stares back at me. Exhales. Stares back again. The fingers holding her cigarette are two yellow batons ready to lead me in the right direction, her direction. In her smoke, each white puff is a paragraph of her yesterdays. Paragraphs grabbed by wind. Paragraphs scattered like angel hair.

Then she faces me. I'd better listen to her life.

"I remember best, angling down the street at age twenty, with a definite spring in my legs," she says. "My hands were fisted in my coat sleeves and clenched with the little money I had. I could smoke and speak at the same time. I want a cigarette to glow forever from a twenty-year old mouth," she says.

From her younger mouth, I see nothing but angel hair puffing out, reaching for sky. She seems unaware of her seventy-to-twenty-to-seventy custom. The grabbing wind repeats her habit for me and the clouds are jealous friends.

The Ostrich Wears Glasses

Nobody feels sorry for Jill. Death. She pretends she's close to it. Not real death. Just toughness. I am reporting her every last breath. Then, Jill quickly drops her head again, as if she wants to continue telling how hard-assed her life story has been to an audience of worms; a sympathetic audience can only come from under somewhere. Certainly not from above ground.

"I don't bleed over anyone or anything," she tells me one day after work.

"Are you auditioning for a Clint Eastwood movie?" I ask.

"Death is an eager gunfighter," she says.

Maybe Jill would secretly love to be preyed upon by a thousand imaginary insects. Provide her skin with new pores, new tunnels.

Last week, she apologized for showing her emotions: two women workers made a big financial decision on their own and this made her nervous.

"Why don't you take off your glasses so I can clean them for you?" I offer.

As Jill moves her hand towards her face, ants freeze in their task of colonizing her lips and tongue. I hear the queen ant laughing at Jill's strange power and, when the laughter stops, Jill finally removes her glasses and hands them to me.

"Try turning around, Jill, with your back to me. Don't move a muscle!" I say.

"Are you ordering me around? Don't forget who I am around here!" she says, turning her back to me.

"Right," I say. "Right."

I watch her skirt and then her blouse ripple as platoons of ants and worms work their way up her spine.

MONKEY PUZZLE

I beg to be touched. They beg to be touched. The Monkey Puzzle Trees near The Lion's Gate Bridge here in Vancouver are toxic. But I am not ready for a nauseous moment.

Next to the trees, I meet a woman who says:

"I sometimes sell myself to men who visit The Monkey Puzzle Trees."

Yet today she seems more attuned to studying vegetation than getting some business going with me. Her thighs may go on forever, but she reminds me of that modest English bather who wears a terrycloth bag over her body as she quickly changes into her swimsuit. Maybe the woman touched the Monkey Puzzle Trees before I arrived here.

"Life on the streets is a life that started out of necessity. And those johns ... one time this guy fell in love with me after ten minutes of sex. I told him I used to be a botanist at the university but the plants got to me. I nearly went crazy when the man proposed to me over and over again. He wouldn't stop. But why am I telling you all this?" the woman finally says into my face, her breath smelling like stale coffee.

"I don't know," I say.

I beg to be touched.

LIGHT BREATHING

She's in love and I'm in love with her loving.

In the bar, the entertainer performs on her accordion. Her eyes are half-closed, as if she were wishing her fingers to belong to the world. My ears are huge question marks: who does she want? who does she want? Whether the crowd understands or not is of little concern to her. But, gradually, her music invites me to her chest. After each note, her lips move, as if they plan to set fire to a lover described in her songs, to her possible lover in the front row. Earlier, the entertainer told me that this is her way of slowing down the revelation of her character flaws so she can have her pick of potential lovers. During her last break, she walked by my table and suddenly asked me, a stranger:

"Why do lovers always strut their best behavior during courting?"

"You think I know about that," I say.

"You should," she says, her voice like the finest sandpaper.

Right now, the entertainer exhales love for everyone here. The breathing in the bar is so so light...I hear the ice cubes in my glass.

IV
TRADES

Vegetables And The Butcher

The tall, wiry man is a blood-aproned butcher but has never eaten a full plate of meat himself. However, the day is not far off when he will do it.

Today in his shop, he has one hand on the thigh of a cow and the other grips a huge knife. One man and two women enter and immediately lecture him:

"How can you be so cruel to animals?" the man protests, as if he were an over-aged boy scout.

"Your view of nutrition is narrow!" one of the women says, her intensity, like the dry, cracked skin on her forehead.

When the butcher shows his nonchalance, the vegetarians rant and rave until their necks and faces are lined with red thermometers of heart.

He grins his apron string grin. Waits until they've pushed too far. Then he demonstrates how sharp his knife is by slicing a sheet of wrapping paper into threads on the chopping block.

"Watch this," the butcher smiles. "Pay attention!"

Then he shifts the knife's handle between his thumb and forefinger.

"Think of having vegetarian steaks sliced just right for you in the produce department," he says.

That makes the vegetarians drop their cabbage heads and flee.

Later, in a bistro, the butcher tells me that he sees vegetarians as gutless: "Those idiots push themselves much much harder than the people they aim at."

Finally, he becomes that farmer who moves to a table to drink with friends where it is suggested they all strip naked and test their strength. First, they hit each other over the head with frozen turnips grabbed from the kitchen, but then one man staggers outside, seizes a chain saw from his truck and cuts off his own foot. Not to be outdone, the butcher grabs the saw, shouts "Watch this then!" and chops off his own head.

THE PINK CAROUSEL HORSE

Today I am a carousel maintenance man and I feel like I'm holding onto something dearer than my own life. The leather bridal in my grip belongs to my favorite animal, a pink carousel horse, the softest yet hardest of my memories.

I've just finished spray-painting the animal, except for its left iris, which has been worn away by riders' hands. The rest of the horse looks as if it never left the front of a store. And my hands are spotted with a deeper shade of pink. Since my last task is to fix the horse's iris, I practice my painting skills in the sunlight before making a move with my brush.

I imagine doing the same thing to my own dog. He would probably just rest there on his haunches, with big, wet eyes browned with trust. But my dog's eyes don't ever need coloring so my hesitation is understandable. Such a detail of eye is significant.

Then I begin. The inhaling faces of children move in and out with my delicate paint strokes. In the air, the acrid smell of paint cuts across the sun's fingers. At the tip of my brush, the smoothness of enamel, almost hangs, waits. My eyeball dabbling with a feather. Later, I stand back, as if making sure the carousel horse looks as real as possible. I examine my strokes. The horse now has a promising look only carousels can keep.

"I want my horse to have but one flaw. A tiny flaw. A missing eyelash. Visible only to me. It's only human, you know, to have at least one flaw," I say to the children.

Behind us, a barker practices his voice and I smell a hint of burnt popcorn.

Scream

After crossing her fingers and wishing aloud that she be chosen, the woman in the cherry red pant suit blows all her hope into a giant red circus balloon. Sure enough, the ringmaster selects the woman and her balloon to volunteer for the main ring, and she is left lip -frozen by her own screaming, her delight.

In the ring, the woman reminds him that she sees herself as a noiseless performer but her mouth has more words than teeth. And the strong smells of animals makes the woman's nose scan the crowd, searching for another face to live on.

"Please hold these two hoops for the monkeys to jump through," the ringmaster says.

Then a few heads from the crowd nod in a way that says the woman has performed here before. When she closes her eyes, the woman looks as if she is whispering into the ringmaster's ear that the cheering for her efforts must be coming from outside, faraway from this circus tent, perhaps from herds of horses, grazing in a fog-filled field. The sounds of the horses' nostrils are tiny air holes. Small muscle vents. Pushing one by one at the woman's chosen wish.

"You can't be cheering for me," she says directly into the microphone.

Her fingers are still crossed when she opens her eyes and she is amazed at the curl in her thumbs.

Holiday Fingers

The surgeon can't sleep. He leans into his exhaustion with a coffee cup in hand, frozen by the results of the slow-breathing operation he completed just minutes before. The surgeon's hands, which have forgotten how to sweat, seem more numb than any other part of his body and they could belong to a mannequin.

When he studies his hands, the surgeon realizes they need to be sent to a faraway South Seas island for rest. There his hands will bask in the sun. Sometimes, they will float on the ocean or thrust their strain into the warm, warm sand. Other times, the hands will sleep into noon's heat until the fingers need not be responsible for anything or anyone.

After the hands return to the surgeon's arms, he puts his coffee cup down and holds the hands up to the cafeteria light. There is still sand in spaces between his fingers. Perhaps the fingers are friends who needed time to be alone. Sleep. Sleep. Sleep.

"Thanks for your silence," he suddenly announces to everyone.

Others in the cafeteria look, whisper possibilities for his behavior: "Long hours. Stress. Fatigue. A patient lawsuit. Failed marriage. Sex. A troubled son."

The surgeon orders another coffee and asks a woman colleague: "And when did YOU last sleep?"

"I don't remember," she says. "Maybe on my last vacation."

And the holiday doesn't last. Each of the surgeon's hands study each other and slump on the counter, like two exhausted families from a Third World country.

From the ceiling, a voice calls.

Two Cents On Hunting

The piano player forces himself to chuckle, as if he were being paid so much per laugh. From a nearby table, the only customers in the bar tell stories and jokes about hunting.

"Did you hear the one about the moose that faked its own death, got up, and then chased its hunter over a cliff?" one patron says.

The piano player congratulates them on their humor. Wants the patrons to listen to his own ideas about hunting. He stops his piano playing. Slips through the cigarette smoke over to their table. Reveals that his own hunting taste is stalking an animal with no gun as per the animal's request. A customer gets serious and says:

"You better take your animal rights somewhere else. And how can an animal possibly request how it will die?"

"Some animals might prefer the quiet of bow and arrow hunting, where death has a precision of its own. Isn't death more clean-cut that way?" the piano man says.

"We got ourselves a philosopher piano man," someone says.

Then the patrons change the subject. Time to study the menu.

"Hey, Piano Man, what would you suggest for supper?" But before he can reply, they say:

"Play us YOUR favorites, Piano Man. YOUR favorites. Show us your stuff! Make us all die from laughing. Again."

A waiter interrupts and asks:

"What'll you have... gentlemen?"

Ballad Of The Tin Can

On the assembly-line the worker shrugs and calls himself a robot. His arms, his legs...all of him belongs to this corporate strangeness.

"Fridays are the days I'm most bored," he says to me. "That's when I sometimes toss empty Coke cans into the fenders of Special Edition cars and weld them shut. Then me and my buddies make fun of the rich owners cursing the whereabouts of rattles."

And today, after completing his Friday ritual, he receives a phone call from a medical clinic telling him that his sperm is too weak for his wife. Then, he calls his wife and sounds as if he were crying her the news.

"Don't worry. Don't worry. I still love you!" his wife says reassuringly.

But he does worry, especially about all the other noises inside his head . Reproducing noises. When the worker hangs up the phone, he says to me:

"Know something? I felt much safer as a kid. Then a tin can didn't make noise on its own. I had to throw it against something. Fill it with small rocks, nuts, bolts, screws. Tie a string to it. Or even crush it. Then, the tin can was my friend. I could make it do whatever I wanted to."

At home that night, the assembly-line robot with diluted, weak sperm plops himself in front of the television and stares at the fake fireplace of his day.

"I still love you. But do you love me?" his wife asks, her voice sounding as it belonged to his mother.

"And now a word from our sponsor," the television says.

HEAD UGLIES

On Monday morning, the boss arrives at work with a head full of uglies. All weekend long, his neighbor drank loudly to the world's health:

"Nearly called the cops three times," the boss says.

But he didn't. Mainly because he knew he had to live with that neighbor after the hangover set in. Twice the boss took out his rifle. Loaded it. Prepared to blast the drunk next door out of the neighborhood. Finally, the boss wrote a story about it, hoping the tale would remove his resentment, like a leftover scab.

He thrusts his story into my hand expecting me to read it carefully. Now.

The story tells of a drunk being shot in a dubious hunting accident in someone's front-yard.

"Read my story a second time", the boss insists.

When I hand him back his story, the boss' eyes become bathed in spit, probably because I don't say much one way or the other.

Then the boss grits his teeth.

"You probably think I'm lousy with words," he snarls.

"No," I say. "Of course not!"

I take back his story. Fold it. Slip it into my jacket pocket. "I'll reread it more carefully tonight," I say. "Away from here. By myself."

Then, I head back to my work. Give a thumbs-up signal to the boss. Point to my jacket pocket. Pat his story. Wish it luck under my breathing.

When I lean over to the desk next to mine, to read the front page of The Globe And Mail showing our Prime Minister, Jean Chretien, inspecting Canadian troops in London, England, the overstuffed clipboard on my desk slips and falls to the floor sounding like the hardened skin of a flat, wooden corpse.

BOXES, BOOZE, FLOWERS, STAMPS

It's Friday morning. I realize my co-worker is close to me and hear his distinctive quickness, that swishing and thudding of boxes being stacked upon each other. The smell of sweat. My co-worker doesn't drink, smoke, or say much. The harder he works, the wider his quiet smile spreads across his face, like parting clouds. Explaining is something his happiness never needs. After work, the warehouse men will go drinking but not him.

"I'd rather grow flowers and collect stamps than hangovers," the co-worker says.

And at coffee break, my working partner pulls out a stamp album from his locker to show everyone. I watch his eyes study the frozen half-smiles or non-smiles on each stamp. Not a reckless grin anywhere! Just Prime Ministers and the Queen.

"Did any of your stamp faces smoke, drink or work as hard as you?" I ask.

But, the co-worker seems to not hear me or my joke. Instead, he holds his own graceful, bony hand up to the sunlight and I realize I'd think nothing of asking that hand to thrust itself through iron bars to water flowers on my father's grave.

A Cast

The bouncer moves like fresh tar around the outside of the tavern crowd. He rubs the cast on his forearm and rereads the autographs and messages.

"You'll be back swinging in no time," said one message. "Must be hard on you," said another.

Then the bouncer flashes his rehearsed bouncer grin and stops at a table. A woman customer complains into his ear:

"See that short guy in the blue suit over there? Well, he burned my hair with his cigar. See. Look at this."

Sure enough, I notice a black spot, the size of a nickel, just before the woman's red hair touched her shoulder. Seems that the short man had been bragging about drinking his beer from buckets and his animated cigar burnt the woman's hair.

Now the bouncer has his cast jammed against the short man's ear.

"Go apologize to that woman. Or you're out of here," the bouncer says.

"Look. I'm sorry. It was an accident," the short man screams.

"Do it anyway!" the bouncer says.

The bouncer removes his cast from the cigar smoker's ear which turns from white to red again.

"That's better, sir," the bouncer smiles. "Thank you very, very much!"

Meanwhile, the short man studies bubbles escaping from the bottom of his glass. His cigar smoke is blown quickly and smoothly into the tavern air. A hand bringing the beer glass to his mouth, is stiffer than the tabletop.

From an open window, the smell of hot oil floats inside to mingle with the odors of beer, food and smoke.

THE FIRE WILL NOT WAIT

Diane smells smoke. Creeping halfway down the stairs, she is so scared her stomach tightens into a perfect frowning face, a face identical to hers. Then she notices flames licking out at her from the kitchen. Diane's huge feet freeze in her pink fluffy slippers. One of her legs protrudes from a nightie and looks like the trunk of a prehistoric beast. The other is rigid against a railing. The rest of her from the waist up is not clear because the flames cause her features to become a wrinkled photograph . Diane might be safer if her head were to fall through her neck and hide in the safety of her stomach. She has to do something, anything with the ice in her blood. She can't stay here forever in the smoke. The fire will not wait. Diane's face. Burning. Freezing.

A fire truck arrives. The front door is smashed open. Two firefighters emerge from a wall of smoke, like seals from a gray sea. They notice Diane's pink slippers on the steps and search the smoke above her head. She recognizes one of them as a former lover:

"Hope you don't think I'd let myself go up in smoke, just because you left me," she says to her ex-boyfriend.

Above everyone, smoke cradles the ceiling with enormous grey hands and waits.

SORTING

I am a circus performer with another line of work. First, I stack one table upon the other, leg to leg, like credits at the end of a movie, until I build myself a tower. I climb to the sixth table and lower myself gingerly into my portable chair.

Then I juggle three red balls, as if sorting letters for the circus audience.

Below, my toy poodle begs, like an open mailbox, to have his mouth filled with one or more of my letters. On their way down to the dog's mouth, the balls become gasps from the audience. If they breathed any louder, my poodle would choke from the noise.

"Did you know, ladies and gentlemen," announces the ring-master, "that our performer used to be a mailman and brought along the very same poodle for company? His act is a natural follow-up to delivering letters."

The audience gives me and my dog a standing ovation after the third red ball is caught between the poodle's teeth. Like a basket of wool with a life of his own, my dog flips his grey and white body through the air turning the main ring into a torna-do of fur and paws.

When the act is over, I grab the ringmaster's microphone and announce my own encore, making the crowd hold its breath like never before.

Will someone ever write to me?

V
NIGHT NET

WHAT THE HEART MIGHT HAVE DONE

(for Lap)

She's been stood up. Ten p.m. Christmas Eve. Montreal. 1940. The seamstress leaves home for the dance hall on her own, as if she were going on a safari for a new man. There she meets friends and a man who's dressed in a zoot suit with wide, wide shoulders. The man's a tailor by trade and he'd feel skinless without a necktie and a clean white shirt. They dance together all night, minds glued to each other's words. Towards the end, he asks the seamstress if she'd like to come back here tomorrow night with him and she agrees with a smile as wide as a Christmas wreath.

When the tailor and the seamstress meet at the front entrance of the dance hall the next night, they wish each other a Merry Christmas without even a handshake and both don't know what to do with their arms and hands. They take an equal number of turns to wink and nod at each other before entering, like the beginning of an eye-to-head-to-heart ritual.

The twelve-man orchestra plays forever. The tailor and the seamstress choose to sit in the balcony and sip their five-cent Cokes. No booze. And tonight, there must be two hundred and fifty dancers on the floor. Later, dance prizes consisting of an alarm clock, a wristwatch and artificial hat flowers are awarded.

"My second alarm clock," the seamstress tells him.

The music doesn't allow the couple to talk much. Dance. Dance. Dance. Hearts. Skins. Warming up. For something. And they never think of changing partners. Ever.

After a few weeks of nightly dancing, the seamstress and the tailor cut back on their dance hall dates to save on streetcar fare. They stay at her place and talk: sleeves, cuffs, waists, lengths, fabric, buttons, thread, prices, sewing machines, customers and laughing lies. Yes ,even lies:

"When the customer says she has a big stomach, I always tell her that she's long-waisted," the seamstress says.

"Last week I had to measure a boxer for a suit. His neck, arms, chest and thighs were so huge that a normal suit would not fall properly on him. This guy wanted so much to be normal that I had to tell him that he was uniquely normal. He believed me."

Listening to records such as STARDUST and IN THE MOOD, the couple sip watered-down Jello powder. And there is something the seamstress wants to tell the tailor. Each time the tailor comes calling, he brings her chocolates, flowers or magazines. She is not a reader, does not have a sweet tooth, and her poverty wants to ask him to instead bring clothes such as a nightie, a dressing gown or pajamas. Takes her eight months to ask him. Takes the skin of her heart that long to reach the same size as that pair of satin pajamas she saw in a store window yesterday.

Right after STARDUST and their second cup of Strawberry Jello, she will ask him.

ON THE NUMBERS

The deception of Time helps me to imagine being retired.

Both my wife and I cling together like tired flowers on the sidewalk outside our apartment complex. A terrible fire has gutted our building. Our joint crying is muffled by the screaming fire engines racing to the scene. We have lost just about everything to the fire. My wife's scarf clings to her head and becomes the flag of a tiny, desperate refugee child I saw on the six o'clock news. With eyes the size of brass buttons from her coat, she grasps a purse that looks like an ancient boxing glove. Meanwhile, I hold on to my only suit and my wife's two best dresses. Not one firefighter asks me about relaxing my grip on the clothes. Nobody asks about the chalked hopscotch digits on the sidewalk beneath our feet.

Over morning coffee, we had a conversation about that high cost of living and all the usual sad jokes about having to eat cat food.

"Will we both grow tails and lick ourselves clean?" she asked me with half a laugh.

We are glued to the numbers. Exhausted white numbers. We are a couple of tulips yanked out of the ground. And our petals are pressing against the grey-white smoke.

"Would you like some coffee?" a fireman asks.

BEASTS AND BABIES

Elisabeth's voice makes me think of cream pouring slowly over my morning cereal. As my breakfast soaks itself, I want to absorb the early day quiet because I am a person made for mornings, the smells of toast, coffee. But my oblivious behavior bothers Elisabeth. She wants to talk. Talk. Talk. When it occurs to her that her voice irritates even the morning sun, Elisabeth becomes a child, wailing in her small way, almost apologizing to the sudden, sunrise face at the window.

Then I remove a pink dinosaur toy from the cereal box. Elisabeth watches me run my finger up and down the animal's spine. Under the dark stream of her hair, I see Elisabeth nursing her loneliness better than I ever could and I secretly envy her.

Elisabeth sprinkles cereal into her bowl, as if she were trying to out-will the world and blows her determination out of the side of her mouth, like some kind of cock-of-the-walk.

"I'd like my cereal to be as soggy as yours," she says.

Right away I fall into the middle of a soggy contest with her. More milk. More spooning.

"And you wonder why I think you have the imagination of a doorknob," I say.

"And why is it only YOU who wonders why my mouth is inversely proportional to my height," she says.

When we get to that place where beasts meet babies, Elisabeth and I will have no choice but to explode at each other and take turns being the beast, the baby. A new carton of milk will splash open its white on the kitchen table because it will not open with our fingernails and requires a knife, just a knife.

Living Help

At this very moment, Thomas' sky is an open mouth filled with a giant tongue, a tongue that seems to say:

"Stay calm, stay... calm."

But Thomas continues to plead with the sky:

"I'm afraid to stop talking because that makes me contemplate suicide. Makes me feel trapped in a dark room whose four corners are filled with dishonesty, fear, resentment, and selfishness. I feel like that shopper in a parking lot who needs to heave against a hundred shopping carts to move them out of the way, a conscientious consumer. Bargains. Death bargains. I've read suicide books and I wouldn't mind using one of those ideas. Maybe, I could turn myself in for the crime. Ha! But would my wife understand? Each time I threaten suicide, I am a harmless kitten soon to be a raging tiger inside my head."

But each time Thomas promised to kill myself in the past, his wife told him it was too easy that way, as if suicide were a way of leisure.

And tonight Thomas' wife is exhausted from his oaths:

"Go ahead, Thomas. Do it. Now. Here, I'll pack for you. You've run out of help, Thomas. From me. From everyone. Come on, do it! Do it!"

Thomas' sky is an open mouth.

SPAGHETTI, KEYHOLES AND SAMMY

"You don't know how to make love anymore, Sammy," his wife suddenly announces from her pillow.

As she natters on and on about Sammy's inability, it's as if his wife is preparing to pack him into a suitcase and send him off to a loveless island somewhere.

"She's probably right," Sammy whispers to himself.

In his new apartment though, Sammy finds another woman who has little use for pillow tallies.

"This sex stuff... for me, it's the greatest equalizer there is," she says. Nobody has to be better or worse."

The new woman is unlike Sammy's wife, who became a frozen fish on her best days.

Sammy says to the new woman:

"I often felt like a seal or a morose sea lion during foreplay with my wife."

A few weeks later, just when Sammy is learning a new bed comfort, his wife declares:

"I want you back, Sammy! Let's give it another try. And as soon as possible, for the good of the kids."

So back he goes, firmly convinced that everyone sees him as his wife does anyhow.

"That other woman was probably just infatuated with me, anyways. Besides, I'm certainly able to soak up the spills of my marriage, so to speak," he tells himself in the bathroom mirror.

During Sammy's first night back, he is impotent again and feels like he's trying to stick cooked spaghetti through a keyhole.

"Not again," his wife says. "Just concentrate, will ya!"

Sammy allows his wide-awake thinking to take him to a brothel he remembers from a movie. There Sammy and that other woman from his apartment re-write a slow motion message on each other's skin. And she teaches him how to spell other words than cry.

WATERTON LAKE HIGHWAY WOMAN

"Look! Look hard! ," the woman beside me says.

She pulls over and points to the highway that looks like a tin strip. Then she slips the car into drive and informs me that the highway is only there to reflect everyone's occasional wisdom.

"Wisdom? What does wisdom have to do with a highway?" I ask.

"Keep your eyes open," she says.

When we reach a turn, we see two bikers cruising side by side. The bikers ride on each other's reflections. The taller biker studies the woman with a tender but thorough look. Everyone accelerates again. The woman slows down. The bikers slow down. We pull over onto the soft shoulder. The bikers do the same.

"Those bikers don't scare me," she says.

Her eyes look up, as if they were scooping up handfuls of sun and cloud.

"Those bikers don't scare me," she says a second time.

"Are you trying to audition for a Sylvester Stallone film?" I ask.

"Watch this", the woman says.

She gets out of the car and flings her lit cigarette at a biker, as if the cigarette were a star tied to a safety line. One of the bikers is an ex-lover of hers. She jumps into his arms and wraps her legs around his body. Legs and arms in a leathered sun.

I watch the highway trying to live with the erratic shine of its ways. The heat from the woman and her ex-lover outdoes the sun. An automobile at the farthest highway hump appears to roll up the tin, like carpet. Yet, that same vehicle also seems to be going nowhere.

"Ready to go?" the woman suddenly asks.

So What If Gophers Skipped On Her Skirts

Please. Not again. Not that story about the young prairie woman waving and talking to laundry pinned across a sensible horizon on wash day. I already know that her clothes talk back when she wants them to.

The grey blanket is her father and his words irritate her, calm her:

"I don't know why you dream so much and I hate dreamers," he says.

The sheets are her mother and they slice up the sky with the intricacies of women:

"Know why a man has a hole in his penis? Because his brain needs oxygen."

Different colored socks are her children blowing every which way:

"Gimme! Gimme! Gimme! Let me walk all over your sky, Mom!"

Underwear are the secret places she hopes to visit. Paris. London. Madrid. Rome. Mysterious accents in the wind.

But I hear the woman saying she doesn't want that huge canopy to wrap her up and take her to a place of bigger skies.

"I'll bet there are no bigger skies anywhere but my husband ignores me," she says. "He tried to share that sky of mine in the same way he once tried to share a Reader's Digest article on a Sunday night. At the time I was puzzled by his offer to share. His attempt at intimacy felt the same way his hands do in bed. You know, like one hand was a stranger to the other."

So what if gophers skipped on the woman's skirt. I want to know who owns her blood. I need to understand why the skin has been gnawed from her heart, as if she had been bitten by a poisonous rodent beforehand.

INKBLOT

(for Lap)

It starts with ink on the pocket of his shirt. Both Louis and the widow are to go to the Do-Re-Mi dance hall for a seniors dance. Right after he arrives to pick her up with ink on his shirt, the widow sends Louis home to change, as if the ink were from a wound in her heart.

"Take a shower too," she says.

An hour drive there and back. While she awaits his return, the widow telephones her only son. Tells him about the inkblot, Louis' need for a shower.

The son says:

"Bet you'd make Louis go stand in the middle of a carwash and let the brushes do their job before each date."

"If I had to, I would," she says.

The widow laughs at her son's idea but becomes red-faced when she hears her doorbell ring. Louis is back. Showered. Clean shirt.

When Louis walks in, the widow takes a quick sniff and peeks under each of his lapels. Clean as a brand new heart.

When they leave, she asks:

"Ready to dance the night away?"

Louis pauses. Inspects each of his armpits, his jacket, his white shirt..., his necktie, his pants, his socks, his shoes. Everything.

"Now it's my turn," he says.

The phone rings.

Lawn Chairs And The Party

At Monica's party, her last booze party, lawn chairs become liquor wombs. Tongues loosen. Brains tighten. The softest thing about Monica, a recovering alcoholic, is her teeth. Teeth that fit together like a puzzle. Teeth leaving few clues why the air turns black at her party. But the same air is probably just music coming from an unwanted passing parade.

"You know how parades box me in. And I want to get rid of every last drop of alcohol in my house," she says to me. "I wanted this final party to cut myself off from my so-called drinking friends. As long as I had booze or bought the next round, these people were always my friends. But when the booze and money disappeared... ."

The more Monica's guests don't make her the center of attention, the more she ebbs with serenity from granting words waiting, waiting, like a mantra, in the pit of her stomach.

And when Monica glances at me, her first friend of sobriety, she says:

"Funny how I saw you right away as that person who has but one lie. You know, the way you like to deny you've been sleeping when awakened by my late night telephone calls. Especially if you're with a woman. Please don't lose your lie. It's the only one you have."

Each lawn chair is now a carefully-shaped yellow matrix. Cool, two a.m. braided plastic walls. Aluminium arms. The booze runs out. Friends leave with their moon tongues flapping in mouths of stars.

"Will you help me clean up after? she asks. "I need to let go of something."

AFTER THE KILL

My kitchen has been invaded. Plastic cups. Two empty glasses have bottoms, like eyes of rust, as if the glasses were competing for ugliness with a nearby bowl of over-ripe fruit. All other glasses and cups are partially filled with scrunched up wet napkins, cigarette butts, and leftover booze. And wait, what's that? My kitchen counter is a prairie of resting buffalo herds lost on their way to slaughter. Carcasses from last night's hunt over-populate my morning.

"Wooee, let's go find us some animals," one man yelped last night.

"What do you mean? We are animals. Party animals!" laughed a young woman, her long red hair springing out of her head.

"Mammals. Not animals. Mammals are what we are," announced a middle-aged school consultant who borrows YOUR watch to tell YOU what time it is, or who knows seventy-eight ways how to make love but doesn't have one person to do it with.

Night. My night deadened by stars. Now, I smell the stale bones of death. Open a window. Let the sun warm the leftovers and dry last night's bones, especially the see-through bones. Bones. I want them as far away from the food processor as possible before the school consultant suddenly awakes and threatens to do something with her own words. Bones.

Outside my open window, I feel the sun warning me with its harsh eye and I hear two children arguing about a skipping rope. Then I smell freshly cut grass.

SENTENCES

(for P.G.)

"They're not mine," I overhear the woman swimmer saying to her much younger woman friend.

On the noon hour beach, the older woman studies a set of footprints. From her chin to her chest, the woman's skin could belong to a lizard and her voice is one of sandpaper on wood. The footprints are beads of hardened air across the wet sand. They look to be about a size twelve, man's shoes. When she looks over both of her shoulders repeatedly, the woman says she hears her father repeating over and over again:

"Whenever you think you look pretty, you are being vain. Whenever you think you look pretty, you are being vain. Whenever you think... ."

Then I watch the woman chase after the tide or run towards shore in front of the waves, as if she were rehearsing her anger for a dangerous stranger. But in a short time, the woman's rage is exhausted, gone, like the mist caused by incoming breakers. When she searches again for her father's footprints, there is nothing in the sand but exclamation marks from other sentences standing in the way of the sun.

NIGHT NET

Judy wants this night to save her from something. We both talk on a front balcony, our elbows resting on the black railing, like large, white arrowheads aimed at the night. Her words are children, searching for soft, enormous webs before they leap out into the night. She's been rehearsing for life since the day she was born. Rehearsing for who she might be: "My father drove me crazy. He was afraid of everything I did even when I'd go to open the living-room curtains, as if I were going to rip open his skin or something. A nun once told me I should leave and move in with my boyfriend. And so I did."

Each childhood Christmas, was a concern for Judy's father. Each one of his nerves was a cue for the rest of the family to laugh at him. If Judy just thought of either shrieking about a gift or singing Joy To The World a little louder than everyone else, her father would machine-gun her out of her seat with his "DON'TS:

"He's taught me everything I know," she says. "How to walk and talk. How to hide. How to believe I could never think twice."

Then Judy says:

"I have to take better care of myself. Day by day. Imagine, my father has been dead for two years but I still breathe, as if he were squeezing my lungs. Listen. Listen."

Her words slip off the railing and collide with each other in the night:

"I lost a whole night's sleep a few days ago because I wasn't sure how to change the light bulb in the hallway. And you know how everyone makes jokes about light bulbs. If they only knew."

And now she speaks cautiously at the black sky, as if it were the land of the blind where one father eye is king.

" I'd love to be like those people I see on Little House On The Prairie," she says. "And if I keep standing still like this, it will kill me."

A star in a far sky corner is her cue.

" Why couldn't I have the moon, Daddy?" she says to the charcoal clouds.

THE LINES OF ARLENE

If Arlene were any quieter, she'd be buried immediately.

She poses on the ground, cross-legged, her back to the world. Arlene is one huge magnet. There are long wavy lines protruding from her. Even around her feet, there are clumps of smaller lines, as if each of her feet were pincushions brimming with steel. Arlene has something I will never want: she lives for attention but won't show it. So what if Arlene is the subject of a painting that I am studying right now. She painted herself only last week.

"Better than a mirror," Arlene said at the time.

Yesterday she told me:

"The less people know about me, the fewer doors opened and my painting only opens one door."

Secrets go back and forth under Arlene's skin. I can hear the jelly beans of blood blipping through her veins. She is that farm child whose only friends were animals. I once worked with her and she often proclaimed she'd love to be Anne Murray. She also has that "under the skin knowledge" of the world:

"Everyone is so so insecure except me," she'd say. "Look at how that man combs his hair to hide his bald spot. Watch that woman over there who speaks to the floor instead of your face. And that other slump-shouldered man. So so insecure."

Before I leave the room and her painting, I tap Arlene on the shoulder and say:

"I can hear your blood, like Morse Code. Must be your animals. The same one who gave you your big lips."

Outside, the sky bleeds an alphabet of rain down a wall of cloud, and I wait for the fox in Arlene's name to say something secure.

EVERYONE HAS A LARGE INTESTINE
(for L.)

"Everyone has a large intestine," Eloise teases me.

"Beautiful! You've confirmed my suspicions that you're a beautiful lunatic,"I say, the laughter shaking my innards into a sleepy language from a far-off country.

Eloise is tall, almost five-ten, and has green eyes, the color of mint. She always smells more of soap than perfume. Because Eloise believes that everyone should wear only two colors, she has chosen chocolate brown and white for all her clothes, maybe to cover the extra pounds she carries, like purses, under her clothes. And her short, rust-colored hair is now trembling above her laughter, as if an earthquake were about to happen under her scalp.

"Let me open a window. You know how I hate feeling stuffy, especially after a good laugh," she says.

"Go ahead," I say.

Eloise grabs hold of the nearest window and heaves it to the ceiling.

"Ahh!" she says. "Much better."

"I'm going to be off work for a few days. Something's not right with my large intestine," I say.

"Get it fixed," she says.

"I am. Doctor told me I have to take nine days off work and I feel kind of guilty."

"Forget the psychology. Just get well," Eloise says, her smile as wide as her filing cabinet is high. But her advice sounds like it is not hers.

Then, a change happens. Suddenly. Eloise's chalky skin becomes a cartographer's dream to her heart and head. No matter how calm she likes to appear, Eloise cannot stop those red blotches from swelling, spreading from her neck to her face, like slow-moving continents that have been cut adrift. There's Africa and Europe and Antarctica and South America and Australia and North America and Asia. Larger and larger portions of red earth. After each patch reaches her cheeks and disappears under her hair, Eloise drops her head, as if she were trying to bury it in her chest. Later, she slides her knees closer together and cups her hands on her thighs, as if each were cradling a single promise.

"That funeral this morning was hard to take," she says.

Then tears pour over only the tops of her eyeballs and stop. It's as if Eloise quickly opened a tiny door behind each eye, counted and measured each tear, and then slammed each door shut. I lightly touch the veins on her right hand and she murmurs something I cannot hear. Pushing myself up from my chair, I feel the words in my head summersaulting over each other, hoping to make Eloise laugh. Instead I say:

"Want your door closed?"

"No," she says in her librarian voice.

"Everyone has a large intestine," I say.

PURE

1. THE FIRST ENTERTAINER

The first entertainer's knee-length nylon is stuffed with dollar bills. A silver, high-heeled foot perches on a chair, her ankle nearly exploding from her shoe. From her happy face, a missing bottom tooth points to a peacock on her head which is really a feather-filled hat. Four large gold buttons are planted down the front of her dress. The entertainer's perfume wants my nostrils to know that there is joy in the way she earns a living. Her thumb and forefinger shape an O.K. signal for her "all is well" world.

"Is there anything I can do for you?" she asks. "Anything at all?" - as if for tonight, pleasure will only be understood living my life for her.

2. THE SECOND ENTERTAINER

The beads around the second entertainer's neck applaud their roundness and float into my eyes like soap bubbles. Chalk-white feathers cover most of her silk hat. A limp, yellow orchid is ready to droop from her chest, like a rag, and may be used to wipe her brow later. From her wrist, a chain bracelet swells becoming rows of smooth silver teeth. On her middle finger, a silver plate of a ring is a half-closed eye watching white waves crash up on the shore of her black dress. One of her hands digs into her hip and the other rests on a shoulder of the first entertainer. The second entertainer peeks through the first entertainer's O.K. signal. She's been in the business long enough to know when to use her partner's signals. And night after night she can rely on her partner. Night after night, she counts her age backwards from at least forty.

"Well, you heard her, what can we do for you?" the second entertainer asks. "And I need to tell you mister, there's nothing pure in our heads!"

AND THE DAY AFTER THAT

The only sure things about her are the red flowers and green leaves on her dress which are still growing. Then there is the safety pin at the back of her neck holding the dress together between braids of raven-black hair. The woman's eyes fling a harsh laugh at me when I ask:

"May I photograph you?"

I am afraid of the response forming in spit at the bottom of her mouth. The woman's bottom teeth are different shades of decay and they could be shock absorbers to protect herself from all photographers like me. Quickly, I change my mind when the woman tells me with eyes bathed in acid:

"Go away! I want to be somewhere else and I work hard at not meeting trouble halfway. Got it!"

Meanwhile, the leaves on her dress are fading but the purple flowers are glowing, like beets. Approaching me to my face the woman says:

"I plan to wear the same dress tomorrow and the day after, and the day after that."

As I'm leaving, I promise myself to do more exercise than simply pushing my luck. A nearby ditch becomes my foxhole where I stop being an atheist.

FIVE SKINS OF EUROPE

1. TELEPHONE AFTERLIFE

Nothing works. At an underground station in London, I try one telephone after another and waste pence after pence. Then I find one that seems to function. A few commuters gather around me. Listen to the Canadian saying HELLO, HELLO, HELLO into a phone I think works. And I am sure it does because I connect to the woman I want. On the other end, she says:

"ALLO, ALLO, ALLO!"

"ALLO, ALLO, ALLO my Canadian accent says.

"ALLO, ALLO, ALLO," the crowd around me chants in fractured Canadian.

Soon my laughter develops a life of its own. The crowd grows larger. I lose my connection with the woman at the other end. At least she'll know that I can't laugh and talk at the same time. Then I wave the phone receiver in the air. Use it like an orchestra leader and conduct the throng around me in a chorus of:

"ALLO, ALLO, ALLO! ALLO, ALLO, ALLO!

The crowd is huge now. A bobby pushes his way through the horde and asks:

"Excuse me, Sir. What are you doing with that receiver in your hand?"

"Doesn't work," I say.

"But you are causing a scene here, Sir."

"Join in," I say.

Over by another phone, a tall, man of about twenty, hides his belly under his belt and leans against the sky. His black hair is the length of a deserted lawn, and his face is a ditch after a rainstorm. He carries a huge placard that reads: DEMAND

MORE JOBS! ENGLAND IS ALREADY ON HER KNEES, WHY NOT PUT HER ON HER BACK? THERE'S ALWAYS AN AFTERLIFE!"

Suddenly, my telephone rings.

"It's for you," the bobby says to the man with the placard.

"It's for you," the man with the placard says to another telephone.

"It's for you," members of the crowd say pointing to each other.

2. ATTENTION

They have my attention. In The London Toy and Model Museum the miniaturized items hold me very still. Especially a Topsy-Turvy black and white stuffed doll, unmarked with a fabric over-filled head. Made in 1935. Eleven inches tall. When I flip her upside-down, she is a white doll. When I turn her right-side up, she is a black doll. It all depends on my perception of up and down.

The museum curator says:

"The doll was very popular back in the 1930's. Little girls often snickered when it was time to change the diaper. Amusing. Confusing for the girls."

And just as the curator summarizes other visitors' responses to the museum, a Black man of about seventy taps me on the shoulder and laughs hard and loud.

"If you only knew how hard it was to change skins so often back then," he says.

The Black man has my attention. He smoothes the doll's dresses with a touch I barely notice.

Then I hear a toy train moving and its wheels take us somewhere.

3. Fingertips

"I promise," the magician says to me. In the West End of London, the street magician invites me into his act.

"I shall pull you through these steel rings," he declares.

And the rings are not even wide enough to fit around my neck. The crowd's response makes me think of my own trick: I jump through the steel hoops, saw the street laughter in half, and then stun the audience by joining the two halves. But the trick remains hidden, as if it were a source of shame. Then the street magician thrusts an arm through a steel hoop and tugs at my arm.

Laughter. Applause.

"Where are you from?" I ask.

"I'm from nowhere. Don't ask anymore questions, please," says the man of illusion.

After his act, the magician reminds everyone:

"I'm a street performer. Not a beggar."

As his hat makes its rounds, the magician whispers to me:

"I have to work hard at being that mortal who can keep a secret. Even though a mortal's lips may be still, it's easier to chatter away magic secrets with one's fingertips."

A pigeon bobs and struts its way across a line of setting sun.

4. Rituals

(for Melissa)

Rituals do not fool her skin.

At Kew Gardens outside London, a flock of Canadian geese waddle across a perfect English lawn. Every few seconds above our heads, an airplane from one of many countries, prepares to land in London; they wait in a spiral, like a religious ceremony. We guess the origin and never know for sure. My daughter, Melissa, studies each creature, like a sudden plane and bird lover.

"How'd the geese get here?" she asks, her eyes as big as teacups. And those airplanes... so many strange colors."

"No idea about the geese but they seem to be at home," I say.

"They look like the changing of the guard at Buckingham Palace," she says. And her mouth remains wide-open but quiet, as if she were frozen by familiarity. Overhead, we guess:

"Egypt. France. Ireland. Thailand. India. Singapore. Germany. France. Belgium."

A passing elderly Englishwoman overhears and says:

"Very good. Very good, indeed!"

The Englishwoman titters, causing me to chuckle, causing the geese to snicker, causing Melissa to giggle and suddenly we are dominoes of laughter.

Rituals do not fool my daughter's skin.

5. The Pond In Back Of Versailles

The pond in back of Versailles is a comic book place where I can slip away from the other tourists. The bubble over my head says:

"Get away from all this skin. Rent a rowboat. Go observe Louis The Fourteenth's own comic strip from his backyard."

I rent a rowboat, and I am soon treated to the Versailles equivalent of a female Willie Nelson huddled in a winter coat on a bench. Old newspapers protrude from her coat, like bouquets of flowers. The woman Willie hums a western tune through her nose just like the real Willie. A sacred cowboy chant. And her spiritual request is honored as ducks gather near her, one by one, like prayer beads. When I row by, she goes eye to eye with me, her eyes being the same color as the near bottom of a whiskey bottle. Both of us are lost for words. Lost on this comic book page. Bubbleless. Now I could have followed the other tourists into the palace. Made the story easier. But I'd never find these tourists in the real comics. They wouldn't know the real Willie Nelson if he used THEIR noses for HIS songs.

Now my rowboat bobs up and down in the water, as if the boat were made of the wooden arms of a past lover. I sing along with Willie, my own nose tuned perfectly with hers. We sing a sanctimonious song. A take it or leave it pond song.

6. MEETING EVE

The church clock outside my Paris hotel announces each hour with clanging bells. Each ring might be a cue for the church to lower its ear to the Paris streets. Lower. Lower. Lower. Back to Adam and Eve.

When I visit that same church the next day, God asks me to study a woman dancing among the dark empty pews.

"She's Eve. And she's back. I have a loving plan for you and Eve," God says more clearly than any clock's heartbeat.

Later, at the Chagall collection in Place Pompidou, I notice the same Eve at a café table sipping café-au-lait.

"Good afternoon, so good to see you."

"Moi, je m'appelle, Eve," she says.

"I know. May I join you?" I ask.

"Mais oui," she says. "I know who you are."

Soon, Eve is inspecting a bowl of apples on our table; she is famished.

"I am so tired from listening to those church bells all night," I say.

"I want to eat for the rest of my life," Eve says. "I have my own clock and it moves like the everyday rising and falling of flesh. Come. We will make our flesh move faster. You understand?"

"Of course," I say. "Oui."

That night in Le Danton Café, Eve and I paw each other with delicate fingers, always on the verge of magnificent love. I offer her endless apples. She wraps me in the black, black velvet of her night. And that nighttime clock stops dead on its own time.

Tomorrow, the sun will rise only when we do and then test our skins for the dew of love.

7. DUBLIN DERMIS

(For James Joyce)

"You two travelling together?" the custom's official asks.

After we nod, he says: "For now anyway."

Dublin, your narrow, winding streets turn back on each other, as if they are aroused fingers. The opaque loveliness of dirt. Like the beggars who are polite in their starvation, as if restraining their hunger were the only way to get fed amidst the big city smells and noises of cars, trucks, busses, sweat, smoke, garbage, flowers and food - lots of food breathing, breathing, like in Paris, London, Madrid, San Francisco, Montreal. And every fifth building is a pub but some of your people say they are only the second largest beer consumer in the world, meaning only every second baby bottle is filled with Guinness. Pubs. Places where people ask dryly: "And where did you obtain such a well-informed opinion?" Places where cigarette smoke hangs like halos for those Barcelona teen angels, here to learn your Irish English. Places where visitors get baited, tested for debate, for laughter: An enormous horse trots into a pub and the bartender asks: "Why the long face?"

Both inside and outside of pubs, languages fill the blue-ash air with after-rain colors: Red for Italian. Redder for Spanish. Dolphin-grey for German. Blue for English. Bluer for French. Blue-white, almost transparent, for Dutch. And that quiet, almost moody green for the locals. They say nearly half your workers are under the age of thirty. But where are all their mothers and fathers? Women dressed in black and white and grey have tiny, silver crucifixes hanging above their large, honest breasts, which look like they are trying to coax the sun through clouds. Tall, long women in charge of their lives. A city of daughters, a surprising number with the beginnings of double chins. And young men who look like they wished they were older, mostly in dark suits, slide along your Grafton Street at noon and speak without moving their upper lips. A mumbled song showing me new ways to listen. What's that you say, Dublin? Everyone here has a good voice. Not like some of those South Koreans lacking vocal talent who try to improve their karaoke abilities by attending clinics where they sing with blue, plastic buckets over their heads. So you want your men to be a little more sexy when sober. Then show them how, Dublin. Show them how. Maybe grab them by their pants. Insist. Insist. But some of the office workers clasp each other by the shoulders, sing, and then say something from the bottom of their mouths. Little eye contact. Just to drive psychologists crazy. The bantering. The teasing. The God-awful beauty of their laughter, with cell-phones shaking, punctuating the air. I love these crowds of workers and tourists; they massage my skin as they walk by - especially the black-eyed beauty who looks like she grew out of her armful of flowers; I inhale her tulip skin as she walks by; she speaks to both her cell-phone and workmate, back and forth, like a metronome - something about being cut from management cloth. And the Irish skin - as pale as the bread at Mass. Dark hair. Very moody one minute.

Very friendly the next. Very freckled skin with red hair. And you whisper to me, Dublin, saying it's because of rust from the ever-constant light, light rain - all freshly-made over The Irish Sea and Atlantic Ocean. Meanwhile, a guide at your Dublin Castle walks with wooden skin, her mouth is two separate floors of the same building; she is so stiff, I hear her pantyhose creaking around her chalk-white, shiny legs; I listen to her words go ON-OFF, ON-OFF. Words as smooth as newly-capped teeth. But your skin fits me, Dublin. Irish wool is provided to me tax-free because my passport says I am Canadian. The wool smells of life, as if still on the backs of sheep. Wait till they X-ray me. Wait till they X-ray. Me. And in the middle of O'Connell Street Bridge, I look down into Liffey River and the tide is out - the result of a pure Irish moon at work. Moss, looking like green wool, is left clinging to river bank walls - more than enough to knit sweaters for tourists. And in the shallow water, I see the faces of the same Irish women who were on stage at the Abbey Theatre last night; the faces showing how tough it was for five unmarried women and one love-child son living together in a Donegal summer of 1936; women who were cut off from everyone because the Pope at the time said the women would be open to the temptations of men; but these single women made music from all language and could teach the Pope how to sing and dance at the same time. And when I turn away from Liffey River, I see boys married to girls going by me, wheeling babies and more babies, with toddlers tied to strollers, like pets. Boys. Girls. Bypassing adulthood. In case. Just in case they got too old too fast. And on a north corner of O'Connell Street Bridge, a middle-aged man and woman, dressed in black, carry black and white placards displaying dead babies; they stop, twist into fetal positions, saying: "Pray for us, pray for us"; their brows arching up and down in unison with knuckles and fingers slipping from prayer to prayer to prayer. And the skin inside St. Patrick's Cathedral is made of dripping grey stone and stained glass windows tell stories of a medieval God. Shaped like a huge cross, I walk up and down and across the arms and body of Christ imagining my feet as feathers. I think of giving away my only son. My only son. The letting go. And light hangs like mirrors. I see you, St Patrick. I see you. Wooden pews for two classes of people. Where were you sitting, St. Patrick when that mentally handicapped man outside tried to show off how well he could ride a bike but kept falling off when he attempted to ride up two cement church steps and children laughing and chanting: "Pauly, Pauly, Pauly!" And you very recently celebrated your thousandth birthday, Dublin. Well, your pulse is younger than most. Cranes hang over your buildings, like steel sky ribs belonging to a boy's building set. And what about those Vikings who left you here to decompose? Your brain and internal organs remained intact despite the bacteria and insects of time. Your scabs became the opiates of future generations. And Christopher Columbus must be still wondering how he got here. But we'll never be too wry with each other, Dublin. Never. Otherwise, our passion will be gone. Gone. And for the rest of my life I'll be saying: "Sorry! Sorry! Sorry!"- because I spoke while you were in motion.

IN THE CHURCH OF HANDS AND LAUGHTER

1.

The church usher wears a sports jacket that looks like it was sewn on him. And his puffy, curly, bark-brown hair belongs to someone else. As he walks down the aisle, he tries to fold his pious hands but his fingers know better. The usher's shirt is the color of clouds and his tie is as red as a freshly-plucked cherry. Did he borrow his hands from someone for the occasion? Like strangers in a crowded subway, his fingers lean up against each other. They form incomplete tents and half-circles of prayer. Then the usher tries to hold his hands at his chest like fleshy fans but they fumble over each other and slide down his polyester jacket to his belly where they try to lock together, palms facing the world. His face tightens and slackens, as if cartoons poured out of his eyes. When his mouth opens and closes, it asks for a happy face. Suddenly, the usher's hands fall to his sides and he drops his head to the tiled floor, his lips praying for deep pockets. Rightful hands. Where are his rightful hands? When he's in church, the usher thinks of going fishing. When he's fishing, he could be wondering why his fingers do not work in church. And his fishing partner says:

"Laugh from your belly. Not from your tonsils. That'll help your hands, your fingers. And wear mitts in church if you have to. Yea, mitts!"

2.

After the service, the woman at the back of the church says to the usher:

"I hate when people use the word 'girl'!"

"What's the big deal? Weren't you once a girl just like I was once a boy?"

"It's the subtlety of it all," she says. "The implications."

"I like being called 'boy' sometimes. Nothing too serious," the usher says.

"It's politically inappropriate," the woman says.

"Be careful," the usher says.

"Of what?"

"Your panties... they might harden... become rock tokens... then shatter."

"Why do men always have to resort to jokes or sex in an argument, eh?"

"Sex? Not now, lady. Not here!" the usher whispers.

From the back of her throat, her laugh begins and ends. Rehearsed noise. Like listening to an engine pretending to start. She is dressed in purple to hide the extra weight that hangs, like a dozen jelly bean bags from her body. Her long, stringy hair is the color of red licorice and her voice could belong to a travel tour guide. Pea-green eyes narrow in scorn. Hot eyes in slits. Her hands smell of new sweat. Perhaps, they are rented from the hero of her life story, a story of perpetual flooding. Listen to her gasping, to her tonsils talk their way up a telephone pole to safety, her forced laughter tangled in the small purity of the tallest wires.

"Bet I could teach you how to pray your way out of yourself," she says to the usher.

"And then what?" the usher asks.

SONATA

(For Annie)

When my daughter goes for a walk with me, she makes the snow sing songs I thought I've heard before but haven't. Songs of new hearts. Songs of make-believe love. Songs of unsure feet. Songs of long, tall cravings. Songs to make the eyes look anywhere but up. All of these songs crunching and squeaking beneath our feet. I want to memorize the lyrics but their last lines ask me to wait.

She is fifteen. Much taller than others her age. Soft, dark hair, like a halo of night. Eyes as bright and as big as chocolate moons. A brain, a heart both larger than this night. She wants to have a boy care about her but she's not sure how to make that happen.

"The boy in your dad cares about you very much," I say.

"Not the same, Dad. You know that," she says.

"Right," I say.

Curious. Her questions fly from her lips into the icy air, like a school of startled goldfish being poured out of an aquarium into a winter night. Goldfish exploding from her stomach. Her panting from our brisk walking drums against the darkness. And each of her questions is the leg of a winter hare being lifted from her heart, a heart refusing to winterize itself.

"I know very little about relationships," I say. "And that's easy to say because I don't."

But her lips keep moving. My father ears wait, flapping to themselves. She talks, talks herself out. The beauty of words running out of my daughter. The beauty of a daughter running out of words. The goldfish are gone. The air is placid. My daughter's eyes flutter a sonata of hope at her moving feet.

"You haven't said much tonight, Dad," she says.

"Look up," I say, my voice like felt. "Tonight, the sky will celebrate a star called 'You'."